# ATHOS & MILADY

## IN THE
## BEGINNING

# ATHOS & MILADY

# IN THE BEGINNING

## Jennifer M. Fulford

A Romantic Prequel to
THE THREE MUSKETEERS
by Alexandre Dumas

Book Two of The Musketeer Series

Black Bomb Books LLC
Asheville, NC
www.BlackBombBooks.com
blackbombbooks@gmail.com



Interior layout by Maureen Cutajar, gopublished.com

ISBN: 978-0692590966

*For my mother, Carol,*
*whose advice I took this time.*

# I

# FROM GOD, MAN

*Here I lie mournful with desire,*
*feeble in bitterness of the pain Gods inflicted upon me,*
*Struck through the bones with love.*
*~ Archilochus, Greek poet*

# Athos's Log, April 1619

*Men often wonder what their destinies will be. I have never wondered about mine. I have questioned whether mortal men can live rightly by God, in harmony with His requests for purity and the endless pursuit of self-perfection. I know my life is not a shining example. But could it be? My faith says I must try.*

# 1

# The Hunt

A thos whipped his stallion to widen the lead. Several riders trailed him within a horse's length. The vibration of the hoof beats pulsed through him. Dogs barked in the periphery. The open run and the strength of the mount underneath him heightened the competition to pure pleasure. The ultimate goal was to win. The hunt was always about winning.

"Yah!" Athos drove his stallion through the brush toward the red stag. The wind flew by and caused tears to run down his cheek. The wide-eyed stag leaped from point to point, frantic in its final moments.

"Bronte! Go round the stream!" A gesture would have done, but the thrill of a swift kill intensified Athos's enthusiasm. His tactics and those of his hunting partner grew from years of experience. They also shared similar instincts—pursue with blind purpose.

Racing through the woods, the stag seized up at a log, hindering a clean jump. A copper trophy, the stag stood frozen in the spring wind and flared its nostrils in bursts of exhales. Within shooting distance, Athos stopped short, aimed his musket and hesitated.

"Take him," he shouted to Bronte. There was a split-second pause and a shot. The explosion crackled in the air. The buck jerked with the punch of the bullet, and its heavy body staggered and began another short run, blood streaking its front haunches. After five leaps, it crumpled and landed with the impact of fallen timber. The gunpowder in the wind smelled sweet.

Athos waved to Bronte across the woods. "He's yours!"

The hunting party, a half-dozen men and two hounds, circled the dying animal as it took its final, sputtered breaths. Congratulations were short before two servants on foot began the ritual harvest, and the dogs earned bloody hunks in reward. The return trip to the stables was taken at leisure by the riders. The men regrouped inside the stables and exchanged snippets of the morning's adventure and, as always, prodded Athos for another run the next day.

"So you can go home and impress your women? It's spring, men. Save the serious hunting for the fall." He laughed and slapped the back of a young ostler, who looked relieved not to have to repeat his hunting chores the following day. Athos was ready for a demijohn of wine. Better yet, several. Every good hunt, and a few of the bad, called for wine.

Sending the men on their way, Athos invited Bronte inside the Château at Valliere, which he kept quiet by choice, limiting social events. Bronte was usually the only one who joined him in the library, the place they preferred to talk since Athos's sudden rise to sovereignty. Filled with a few fine chairs, a loveseat, a matching chaise lounge, and a study table, it was an excellent place for their dreams of legend-making.

Athos requested his best Argenteuil vintage from the cellar. The aromatic wine and the smell of the books in the study could wind down his most excitable moments.

"I have a new jewel for you," Bronte said after their first sips. The two men had removed their riding jackets and sat in the wingback chairs that overlooked a view of the estate. Three tall, leaded panes looked out onto the estate, which extended far beyond the horizon.

"I reward you with the kill and you try tempting me with a woman again?" Athos playfully shook his head. "When will you learn? Leave the other hunting to me."

Bronte's smile was more of a slant. "You know I'll never stop meddling, especially since you have been without company ... what now? Ten months?"

Athos finished his glassful in a slow drink. "Eight."

"Eight too many."

"My priest says a blessing at every confession," Athos said, one side of his mouth upturned.

Laughing, Bronte raised his glass. "When has that stopped you?"

"I don't throw out morals altogether." The wine was warming Athos's body and his cockiness with it. "I say a prayer of salvation for each and every beauty I've convinced to love me."

"Yes, of course, you pray for their well-being, but your confession doesn't have to disclose *everything*. Save a little for the next one." Bronte patted Athos on the shoulder on his way to the bottle and dropped into the shallow loveseat, stretching across the threaded silk, careful not to spill.

"There must be a poet or three or a dozen on your bookshelves who would go on eloquently about the virtues of lying naked with a woman," Bronte said. "Don't you miss it? After a few weeks, my mouth goes dry, among other things. Use your good looks and get on with it."

Athos couldn't argue about his appeal. His sturdy build, grey eyes and wavy blond hair, always in a tussle, made him look more the part of a Greek god. "I'm selective."

"Selective? You're down-right chaste."

Athos enjoyed being smug and peered through his empty glass toward the sunlight from the window. "It's better that way."

"Sex is essential. And no sex is no good. Doesn't it go against the Psalms or some Biblical passage that absolute purity of the body weakens the soul? In my estimations, God created Eve so Adam would have a warm companion at night."

"Careful, God is listening," Athos said, lifting his glass up.

"Without the warmth of a woman, we shrivel."

Athos crossed over for a refill. "Speaking from experience?"

"You know what I mean."

Leaving Bronte an empty bottle, Athos skimmed over the titles on his bookshelf. He dedicated two shelves to volumes of poems he had found while travelling abroad, evidence of his life as the son of an important man. His hobby bordered on the obsessive. He retrieved a thin book, which opened voluntarily to a familiar page.

"Who is she?" Athos didn't look up.

"That's more like it." In a deft move, Bronte was at his side, cocking his head to read the spine. "Ah, du Bellay. At least he's French. Have any English poets on those shelves? She's English."

"Is she interested in poetry?" Athos pointed Bronte to another thin volume.

"I believe so. An English woman with lips like a rose in bloom and a backside to match."

"Fair enough." Athos respected his friend's tastes in women. Bronte usually chose education over status. Beauty over refinement. Vixen over virtue, the exception being Bronte's true love, Demi. "Tell me more."

The mademoiselle was the sister of the new priest in Averdon, a neighbouring village in Berry, the province Athos now ruled. Young with milky skin, her blue eyes were quick to shine on strangers, and she had made friends with women Bronte knew. They appeared to have taken her on as their pet.

"She's not the ordinary, adorable kind," Bronte said, flipping through pages haphazardly. "She's the kind you worship, the sort of woman you favour."

"How so?" Athos looked up from his book.

"She's smart. She speaks French though she's English. She knows French poetry." Bronte reread the spine in Athos's possession. "She's a delicacy awaiting a connoisseur."

Athos slapped the book shut. "I can take care of my own needs. You may have good taste in women, but your matchmaking has its shortcomings."

"Paris was different. You were mourning your father." Bronte returned his book to the shelf. "But you'd better take steps before the more powerful provincial lords smell weakness." Bronte waved to a shelf of books about war strategies. "You can't afford showing any vulnerability, and your bed could use an ember. This one will send the château burning."

"It sounds as if you've been thinking of approaching her yourself." Athos grabbed a very rare copy of *The Art of War.* "But I strongly advocate against it."

"Yes, love gets in the way of less wholesome pursuits." Bronte rubbed the back of his neck. "I will be making arrangements for a wedding soon, if Demi will still have me."

Athos dropped the book, which landed on the hardwood floor with a clap. "Have I been asleep? I can't believe you're finally committing. I'm wordless."

"You, speechless? My closeted poet?" Bronte said, puffing out his chest, which quickly deflated. "I had to give in sometime."

"You kept saying it wasn't right, but after two years, what could be wrong? I'm proud of you. I had no idea."

"Neither did I," Bronte said. "Demi received another offer, and it's driving me to irrational behavior."

"What kind of scoundrel?" Even Athos knew better than to reveal the slightest flutter of his fondness for Demi.

"Racine." Bronte sneered.

Athos's boisterous laughter caused a servant to stick a head around the door, only to be shooed away. "Very bold, for your brother. I'm surprised you haven't run a blade through him yet."

"He's a fool," Bronte said, catching the servant for another bottle. "It would have been asinine to duel Racine. Besides, she has no interest in him. He may have even proposed to goad me into it. But, she's a prize worth having. I simply need to commit."

"Then we shall celebrate." Athos called the servant back and requested champagne and stationery. If any occasion called for celebration, this milestone did. And it might put an end to his slight envy over Bronte's fortunate matchmaking.

"Don't tell me you're going to write a poem," Bronte said, grabbing a fistful of his own hair.

"I'm drafting an invitation to celebrate your engagement, the first party under my rule," Athos said.

"Hold on." Bronte stopped Athos, who was about to take the wine to the desk. "I must settle the arrangement first."

"And you shall." Athos opened the roll-top and retrieved an inkwell and quill. "Have you spoken with Father Turre about this yet?"

"You know the answer to that."

"He'll be beside himself that you're finally going to marriage."

"I'll only consent to an engagement party on one condition," Bronte said.

Athos laid the quill on the desktop and nodded solidly.

"Meet the English beauty first. Then, I shall propose and you shall have a companion at my party."

"Done." Their handshake sealed the plan.

# The New Mark

"I can smell your hair tonic upwind." Bronte yelled across the dusty roadway, slightly out of breath from the last horse sprint on the way to Mass. Athos had rearranged his Sunday to see the sister of the new priest.

Bronte said her name was Anne de Breuil. He promised the trip would be productive and hinted the mademoiselle might agree to a stroll after the service.

"Too much?" Athos ran his fingers through the layers of his flaxen, chin-length hair. "I can always dunk my head in a watering hole." They laughed and took the rest of the half-hour ride to Averdon at a slower pace, though the anticipation of the endgame—to track a beautiful woman—geared their nerves for sport.

The church was the spiritual home for several villages,

and having a new priest caused incredible excitement among the local peasants. On the scale of life events, a new spiritual leader was an event of great magnitude. An even greater event was an unannounced visit from the new sovereign. When Bronte arrived with Athos at his side, whispered conversations began at once. The local men instantly formed a line to meet the young provincial prince.

Athos used his horse to shield himself from the growing line of admirers and asked Bronte the question most pertinent on his mind. "Is she here?"

Because Bronte had visited the church from time to time to check on its condition and collect taxes, he'd seen Anne on at least two occasions from a distance. So far, he hadn't met her brother, the new priest. "I don't see her."

Bronte spent the next half hour introducing Athos. The blacksmith, a horse breeder, and a vitner bowed awkwardly, all out of practice, then launched into stories that Athos had no choice but to endure. They hand-wrung over taxes, doled out windy compliments, and blustered about rain—the point being to leave an impression on the sovereign, even if a bad one. Athos nodded and smiled, trying to care but battling impatience. Distraction perched on his shoulder.

No one in the vicinity matched the description of Bronte's new mark. After more than a dozen formal greetings, Athos motioned for a break from Bronte, who promised the rest in line an audience later. Then Bronte whisked him inside the church, with a skill he'd perfected throughout their entire friendship. They landed in the baptismal, a circular chamber with a domed ceiling and a shallow oval tank of stone in the centre.

"Sorry, but if you'd start meeting your subjects more regularly, you'd been spared. You're too desirable," Bronte said, less surprised about the crowd than Athos. "Good timing though. Anne's here, across the room."

She stood thirty paces away. Athos knew her without a doubt, as clearly as he could discern a superior silver bullet from lead. Fair-skinned and blond, she glimmered in a crepe gown, reminiscent of a coin rubbed into lustre for the Queen. For a moment, he was mute.

"Your pulse has stopped." Face to face, Bronte tugged at Athos's lapel, pretending to straighten the fold, before he broke into Athos's stare. "You might want to tone down the lust in your eyes."

Athos tried a faint smile. "You're in my way."

She hadn't noticed him yet, the perfect time to drink in every last drop of her. The two young women next to her looked familiar, but their names escaped him. They may have been bright flames, but at that moment the blazing star of Anne outshone them all.

Bronte snapped his fingers. "Don't get ahead of yourself."

"Shh." Athos looked up, tuning into the echo in the room. Voices bounced from the ceiling, transporting conversations from one end to the other. She spoke to her companions, and despite the distance from Athos, her voice was like a chime in a choir. "I can hear her."

"From here? Those damn priests. Always figuring out new ways to find out our secrets. What's she saying?" Bronte glanced over his shoulder. "Tell me. Every word."

"Something about the honeysuckle. She likes the smell of it. It reminds her—I can't believe it." Athos had to look down.

"What? What does it remind her of?"

Athos spoke into his collar. "A lover she took in the grass last spring."

Now, Bronte stared over his shoulder. "You're lying."

"The acoustics are flawless from where I stand."

"Very bold talk for a Sunday morning. Maybe I should talk to them." Bronte started to turn, but Athos grabbed his collar.

"No. Wait." His whisper turned into a plea. "Don't move. They've noticed us. They're laughing."

"At us?" Bronte threw back his shoulders.

"Wait—"

"You're eating all the cake. Let me stand there."

But Athos turned into marble. "She told her friends to look over. Act nonchalant."

Bronte immediately stuck out one hip and ran a hand through his coal-coloured hair. As handsome and fair as Athos was, Bronte was his darker mirror image.

"Not like that," Athos said. But he allowed himself to smile, and for the first time, he made eye contact with her. Her pale blue eyes promised a paradise so genuine that Athos couldn't help but wonder: *Why, God, why did you make her so tempting?* In his mind, there was only one answer.

"I told you she's special," Bronte almost hissed at him, while still peacocking. "You've got that look on your face. Your head's filling up with ideas."

"Things I shouldn't be thinking in church." Athos moistened his lips and wiped the cold sweat from the back of his neck.

"Then you have a lot in common with her." Bronte leaned into Athos. "What are they saying now?" Bronte and patience were never on good terms. Athos had spent more time than he had liked teaching his best friend the virtues of moderation. The fact that Bronte, the independent type, had put off marriage to Demi was troublesome, more trouble than Athos cared to think about now. Athos thought his own virtue could stand a little help, which burned beneath a new sun, *her* sun.

"She's asking her friends our names," Athos said. "You know them? The other two?"

Bronte nodded and raised an eyebrow. "Gossips. The brunette is the daughter of the Marquis de Sigvony. Her name is Genue. She spends the summers here with the other mademoiselle, the cousin of Demi. Margot is her name. Demi tells me her cousin is fond of swimming *au naturel.*"

Athos smiled sideways so no one but his friend could see. Athos was aware his overt attention might come at the price of gossip, so he focused on the crest of Bronte's doublet. Its symbols, a bear paw, a shield, and a fox, represented strength, loyalty, and cunning. Athos's grey eyes began to shine in delight, as if he had just heard the bells of Notre Dame.

"One more thing," Athos said, brushing lint from the crest. He pointed to his own crest, a sword, an eagle, and a dove. "Anne says *your* companion today makes her think of a rare breed of Arabian."

Bronte stifled a lungful of laughter. "You handsome beast. You're in!"

"Not yet," Athos said. "I want to arrange a meeting with her brother first. Shall we?" With nagging persistence, Athos dragged Bronte into the church foyer. Parishioners were crowding into the sanctuary, but the priest hadn't arrived.

Anne's brother, Father Gregori de Breuil, was her guardian, and it was essential that they meet.

"Why bother with him? You already know she's interested. I can tell you're hooked." Bronte jostled a few people to make a break for the baptismal room.

Athos blocked him from the door. He sometimes resented that Bronte had the unnatural ability to read his likes and dislikes. "Hold your Cupid's arrow for now," he said, trying to sound convincing. Except that Bronte was generally right, and this time was no different. Athos was smitten. From their brief encounter, he could pick Anne out of a hundred. *A thousand.* Especially because he'd trained his eye years ago to remember first impressions. Already, the feature he coveted most were her lips. Bronte had described them as a bloom. To Athos, they defied such plain description. They undulated in perfection, two soft peaks, like the side profile of a woman in repose, naked as the dawn.

"What do you know of the priest?" Athos asked, dragging Bronte away from the door.

"That he'll be overjoyed you're interested in his sister."

At the sanctuary entrance, Bronte dipped his fingertips in the holy water at the stoup with an air of indifference. Athos pulled him back into a huddle.

"Yes, but she could have other suitors, men who've secured promises from him. You know as well as I do that a woman that beautiful will attract every eligible man within a day's ride."

Bronte lost his focus at the suggestion. "I know." Then more seriously, he said, "I mean, it doesn't matter too much. Why not have some fun? Like when we were in Paris last fall. You haven't let yourself loose like that since then. She thinks you're a rare breed, so why not take her for a ride?"

Athos shoved Bronte into a corner. "You know me better than that, don't you?"

Regarding women, Athos's ideals had been the subject of many of their discussions since boyhood. It wasn't that Athos lived a virtuous life, but he always wanted his lovers committed to him and he to them, although up to now, never for marriage.

Bronte sighed. "So we speak with the priest."

"It's time for legwork," Athos said, grabbing Bronte's arm. "Find out about her. Who she sees, where she visits. Once I have more information, *anything*, I'll introduce myself to her brother and arrange to meet her. I'm not going into this one blind."

"Very well." He wriggled out from Athos's hold. "Always the strategist. If you'd stop giving advice and listen to mine, maybe you'd recognise it's time you spent a little less time feeding your head and a little more time feeding your body."

Uncharacteristically for a sovereign, Athos and Bronte were among the last to enter the church sanctuary. Because they had been engrossed in plotting, they hadn't seen Anne go in, and the church filled to near capacity. Rather than sit in the front, they found seats near the back, which drew a few strange looks from the locals. But being new and young, Athos simply nodded and looked stern. He wanted the better vantage point.

From the back, Athos hawked the room. Hats and ruffles and lace. The men were just as much to blame for the costumes as the women, although most of the people in the pews were poor country folk adorned in the plainer clothes of their status.

Athos's throat was dry, but his thirst was not for water. *Is she interested in me so quickly?* In the brief connection before Mass, he had learned so much by the way she held her body: she knew the effect she had on men and that made her incredibly self-confident. She loved the attention, and even the women indulged her. She wasn't their pet; they were hers.

She was young. How old, he couldn't tell. If she were too young, complications would abound. His honour was perpetually at stake, and because of his father's recent death, he needed a ironclad reputation. At twenty-five, his age was a constant cloud. He avoided any public event that might portray him as immature; he needed respect more than he needed a scandal with a girl. And as for his faith, he had enough to withstand, especially concerning sin. Thankfully, his past debauchery had been forgiven by his generous priest.

But innocent, she was not. If he hadn't overheard her speaking, he would have known anyway. She was experienced. It took one look to see that she lived a sensual life. *Breathed it.* Had been consumed by the flesh and wanted to be consumed again. In fact, that would be his greatest challenge—to convince her he was enough. If he were the rare horse, she was the wild colt, rollicking and kicking for independence.

From his pew, he spotted her sitting between her two friends. Several locks of her hair fell undone to her nape. She glided a gloved hand up and entwined them on an index finger. She wound the hair tighter and tighter and tilted her head the instant it was too much, then she let go.

Father de Breuil began the prayer from the pulpit. It was from Genesis.

"Let us pray." Every head bowed. Athos watched her. "And there was light. Give thanks to the light. God created Heaven and Earth, and the light made it good. To honour the light is to honour God. I want you to give thanks today to the light that brings us spring again, full of possibilities. The light of God will illuminate our hearts with his love and guidance. There's no greater gift than the warmth of God in our souls. Grace be to God."

The warmth growing in Athos contradicted the prayer. Rather than God, a flame burned within him because of a new temptation.

Worship the light, the priest had said.

Crossing himself, Athos swore to do so by any means possible.

•   •   •

Drenched in sweat, Athos threw his doublet off the moment he and Bronte returned to the horses, fortunate to have escaped another gauntlet of humble-eyed subjects.

"Are you certain you don't want to be introduced to her today?" It was the third time Bronte had asked since the last hymn.

"Absolutely." Athos had one foot in a stirrup.

"Too late." Grinning from ear to ear, Bronte pointed over Athos's shoulder. Behind him a few feet, Anne curtsied, flanked by her two female friends. She covered her face with a hand, failing to hide a mischievous smile. Her friends, Genue and Margot, were a little more composed. Not that they mattered. Athos was too transfixed. *Does she look every man up and down the way she does me?*

Bronte cleared his throat. "Margot, did you see Demi this morning before Mass?"

"I thought you were her keeper now?" Margot giggled. "Aren't you going to introduce us to your friend?"

"Of course. Mademoiselles Margot, Genue, and Anne, this is Comte de la Fere of Berry Province. He's the new sovereign and my very good friend."

"So young," Anne said under her breath toward her companions.

"I could say the same of you." Athos dropped his eyes, trying to regain his tact. "Excuse me for being so rude." He took her hand and lightly kissed the ends of her fingers. "I am called Athos by my closest friends."

"I like Fere better."

"We haven't formally met." Bronte stepped up to Anne, but she gathered her hands behind her before he could take one. He bowed instead. "I'm Bronte."

"My cousin Demi is the target of his affection," Margot said with a jealous inflection.

"Once Bronte is married off, will you miss having him around to play?" Anne asked Athos.

Athos looked Bronte square in the face and communicated with a cocky grin: *I may have found a new playmate.*

"I'll stay busy with or without him," Athos finally said.

Bronte slapped his back with a loud *whack*. "Athos is studying fencing and is a budding poet."

"A poet?" Anne's eyes flickered. "Tell me, who do you read?"

"All the French. Anyone with soul, du Bellay, Marot, Ronsard ..."

"Love poets," she picked up. The others bobbed their heads, obviously clueless. To Athos, her companions might as well have been in the next country.

"And you?" he asked. "Who are you reading?"

"Someone many French have not heard of yet," she said. "Do you know Shakespeare?"

"An Englishman? Never read him," he said.

"He's English, but on a level all his own. He's written 154 sonnets that are very popular with his countrymen. He's—how to best say it—*on fire*."

Athos related. The sweat was dripping down the backs of his knees. He needed to jump in a cool pond, but he could have stood in place and burned the rest of the day away. Anne patted a few beads of sweat from her own lip.

Bronte interrupted. "So it's a date then?"

Everyone looked in his direction, confused. "I mean, you should come and look at Athos's library," Bronte suggested toward the women. "He owns a superb collection."

"Will you have us?" Anne asked Athos.

*I will have you, very soon.* "Of course."

"The day after tomorrow?" Bronte suggested. "I'll escort all three of you."

"And Demi?" Margot asked.

"And Demi," Bronte said, straightening up.

Anne stretched out her hand, which Athos dipped in to kiss, pausing first to look into her blue eyes. Any other woman would have blushed. She challenged him to linger.

"Until then." He brushed her hand with his lips and backed

off, catching a whiff of honeysuckle. The women left as quickly as they arrived. During the ride home, Athos prodded his horse to top speed and outdistanced Bronte by several minutes to arrive at Valliere first.

# Athos's Log

*I suppose my heart deserves wings after years without them. This new woman, Anne, she is worthy, as glorious as the sun, an inadequate description, for words are useless to express my thoughts. The sun was God's gift to the Earth, to make winter into spring, fallow into firmament. He bestowed the light to change the Earth, the very essence of it, from barren to bloom. My eyes could be easily blinded by such light.*

# A New Approach

The next morning, Athos felt as if he had made a mistake. It was too soon for Anne to visit. He didn't know if she was spoken for or entangled in other affairs, either men or intrigues. He had missed an important step: speaking to her brother.

He questioned his judgment. She was a gorgeous creature, and Bronte was right that Athos would find her irresistible. He liked extraordinary women—noteworthy in personality, looks, or tastes—and she fit each category. In personality, she was bold. In looks, the silkiest of cream, and in tastes, she enjoyed his passion for poetry.

But a small voice in his mind said—*take care*. He decided the day before her visit to talk to his mentor, Father Turre. Most Monday afternoons Father Turre took the chance to read in Athos's library, scouring the books on Christianity, enthralled by the opportunity to study.

"Father, may I?" Athos gestured toward the bench.

Seated at a long study table, Father Turre dropped his glasses to his nose. "A problem, my son?"

"Not yet. Well, I'm not sure. Am I disturbing you?"

"No. Sit." Turre poured water from a clay pitcher into a matching cup and put it in front of Athos, who took a seat across from him. "I'm continually at your service and humbly grateful for the use of your library."

"I have met someone. A woman." Athos wasn't concerned about being abrupt. Turre was used to him taking advantage of the excesses of privilege.

"And?"

"She is ignitable." Athos also could be candid. His priest had heard much worse.

Still, Father Turre pursed his lips. "You have been very successful these last few months controlling your more subversive urges. I hope this doesn't mean you're headed in reverse."

"I don't know. I want to be right with God. But how do I do that? Flesh is a powerful distraction, and she may make my will very weak."

Turre gave Athos a faint smile and drew in his hands. "Your father was your age when he married."

"I wish he were still here."

"Every man must find his own path. You need to think less about your pleasure and more about your obligation to his legacy. Since his death, you've been challenged to take on his role, and you've done well. It could be you need to go further, and your lineage as a sovereign is of utmost importance. The longer you go without securing your bloodline, the more vulnerable you are to opportunists. No heir throws many fortunes to the wolves. A more permanent person by your side will strengthen you."

"But I'm only twenty-five."

"Prime age for taking a wife."

"I know nothing of this woman."

"Talk to her parents. Go about it honourably, as you have tried to live so far."

"She's an orphan," Athos said, hesitating. "And English. I doubt she comes with a dowry."

"Oh." Turre tucked his chin and frowned.

"But her guardian is her brother, the new priest in Averdon."

"Oh!" Turre's eyes lit in excitement. "I could inquire for you, if you'd like. He and I haven't met yet, and I would like to."

"She's coming to the estate tomorrow," Athos said. "The plans developed very quickly."

"Well, I can't arrange to meet her brother that soon." Turre placed a hand on Athos's. "Take it slowly. If she seems to be a match, then let it blossom. And think a lot about gardening."

"Gardening?"

"It may preoccupy your mind from more impure thoughts."

Athos mouthed *ah*, chuckling to himself as he got up to leave.

"One more thing," Turre said. "You're a good man. You've made mistakes, committed sins that you have sought forgiveness for, but you're solid. Build on that base. God will reward you for it."

Athos nodded and left the priest to the books.

•   •   •

He met Bronte after dark at a tavern in Blois, a place they went out of boredom. He wanted to prepare for the visit.

"Demi can't come," Bronte said. "She's feeling faint. But the other three are set."

"Will she be well for your engagement party? I'm setting the date for a month from now."

"I meant to talk to you about that."

"No, Bronte," Athos said, waving his hands. "Say you've asked. Say she said yes and showed her appreciation by committing unspeakable acts behind closed doors. Tell me anything except that you've gotten a case of weak nerves."

"Well..." Bronte scanned the dark room of the drinking establishment, trying to shrug off Athos's disappointment.

Athos knocked the bottom of his cup on the table to reclaim Bronte's attention. "What about your brother's proposal?"

"I throttled Racine into submission."

"But Demi deserves your commitment. After two years—"

"When did you adopt such an inflexible moral compass?" Bronte took a long drink and gave Athos a withering look over the rim of his cup. "You, who has *never* committed to marriage. The player who pretends to make each woman his one and only but in reality keeps his heart stashed away inside his château. You do have it locked in a casket there, am I right? I've seen you take that secret passage a time or two, tending to your bleeding heart."

Athos glanced around the tavern to make sure no one heard the insults. "If you weren't my best friend, I might challenge you to a duel right now."

"Then who would you have to kick around?"

Athos emptied the bottle into their cups. "What if I don't seduce her?"

"Backtracking already? I've arranged everything, and now you want out?"

"No." Athos shook his head slowly. "I'm talking about where this might go if we develop a deeper attachment. What if I exercise patience this time?"

"You mean, not bed her?" Bronte laughed as the server walked by, who quickly supplied another bottle. "Why? Granted, you like one woman at a time, but I can't recall patience being your strong suite."

Bronte leaned in, eyes glazed. "Remember Stefania? You had her on her back before the candlewicks at the festival of St. John's Eve were cool. And Yvonne? You took a friendly tour up her skirt the first night, right at the banquet table. I still can't believe I didn't know what was going on, and I was sitting directly across from you."

"You had your face in Demi's." Athos swirled the red liquid left in his cup, remembering averting his own stare from her. "I'm not a lost cause. I need to settle down."

"Not yet, you don't. Your title is too new. It hasn't been nearly long enough for you to exploit it for personal pleasure, not the likes that I would pursue."

"But politics complicates everything I do. Challenges made behind my back in Paris. I'm naive if I don't secure an heir. Beyond your family, few would advocate for me."

"Concentrate between your legs, not your ears." Bronte jabbed Athos in the temple. "Skip the marriage arrangement. She'll satisfy your body, nothing more, and when she does, you'll gain confidence that no political challenger can match. Believe me, I would if I could."

"But you love Demi, and you've had your share, many more than I have."

"I'll never have the position you have. A magistrate's son never trumps a sovereign, even if I buy my title. Take advantage of your power." Bronte shook a fist between them.

"Father Turre wants me to take my time with her."

"Damn him! You have the rest of your life to repent!"

"He says I owe it to my father's legacy."

"Father Turre, this. Father Turre, that." Bronte mockingly crossed himself. "Why don't you just install him in your guest quarters permanently? Marry him!"

Athos slammed his forearm on the table. His anger licked out in a raspy boom.

"I'm a faithful man, unlike some!" He stared Bronte down. "Why shouldn't I consider the higher road? Marriage is a holier outcome."

Bronte waved down the tirade. "It sounds like you don't know what you want."

"I do know one thing," Athos said, the intensity in his voice calming down. "Everything I do is subject to a higher law, whether or not I'm sovereign."

Both called out for more wine. "Of course, of course," Bronte said, "but keeping Anne at bay may be your greatest challenge yet."

•   •   •

The château had to be perfect. Athos instructed his staff to weed the flower beds, trim the hedgerows, polish every piece of silver, beat the largest rugs, and wipe the front windows spotless, especially the grand ones in the library. The bookshelves were dusted, and Athos rechecked the order of his poetry books. Most were French, though he owned volumes from Italy, Spain, and the Netherlands, his collection and gifts from friends who were trying to impress him or his father.

Still, the shelves seemed incomplete. He felt that there was something missing, a little like his life in general. It had been months since his last liaison with a woman for good reason.

At the time, he and Bronte had been staying in Paris and were skipping from fall society gatherings to taverns to parties with the best of the snobs. Beautiful women appeared out of every corner. It was the first time Athos had socialised since his father's death. Seven months after his father's burial, Athos had become a recluse. Bronte had demanded that Athos stop mourning, so he arranged their trip and oversaw the social calendar for the entire fall.

As a best friend, Bronte was the truest, and became so attuned to Athos's subtle clues in body language that they had made a game of it while carousing in Paris. Their first few days, they had refined it: a pinched eyebrow meant *I'm bored*; hands folded below the belt meant *Save me from this conversation*; and running a hand through the hair signalled *Distract everyone so I can take this beauty somewhere private*. At the end of each adventure, usually at the first signs of dawn, they would go over the saucy details of the night, laughing and building the mystique of their manhood.

Because he was the newly anointed sovereign of Berry, his appeal to the opposite sex had increased fourfold in Paris. He couldn't walk into a room without several women, and a few of the men, stalking him from one conversation to the next. His head grew in epic proportion. He couldn't have invented a remedy for loneliness as effective as his new title.

Nonetheless, the temptations compromised his morals. Swimming in luxury and the decadence of Paris society, most nights ended the same: stolen away in some private nook atop a lovely young mademoiselle on the verge of surrender. Typically, at some point in his drunken lust, he'd start wondering if he could remember her name and would reel in his seduction if one didn't immediately come to him. Quite the opposite of Bronte, Athos's excessive wine consumption saved him from many acts of sin. For every disappointed pout, Athos made up for resisting sex by placing several strategic kisses below the navel of his coquette along with the promise of a long love letter.

Near the end of his stay in Paris, Athos knew every nuance of female fashion. Corsets and lace frills and bindings of various purposes and patterns. God had an ulterior motive. Women were more difficult to unwrap than the most complicated Oriental paper folding. The fashions, and his own moral backbone, kept his score sheet of conquests to a manageable minimum.

Except that he had indulged in a virgin. The Duke du Orleans' niece, Simone. She was a red-head and secretly engaged, though the night he plucked her, he was unaware she was engaged. Had he known, his advances never would have happened. They had met, of all places, coming and going from confession at the abbey of Saint Germain de Pres. He had racked up enough sins in two months to keep the priest's ears at Saint Germain burning for another two.

The line for confession that day had been quite long, and he ended up behind Simone. She seemed so innocent, concealed head-to-toe in dark winter clothes, atypical of the other Parisian beauties who used conspicuously bare skin for social favours. She actually told him a joke before her turn. In a coy aside, she said that the only reason the dutiful lit more than one candle at a time in church was to heat up their bones. He saw her two days later at a gala in *le Louvre*. He stayed intentionally sober most of the night, haunting her between rooms crammed with young aristocrats who were hoping to see the King or Queen. She didn't protest his shadowing, and before the night was over, he backed her into a coat room for a long good-night kiss.

He sent her several poems over the course of the next two weeks, astounding himself with a few of the phrases he wrote to woo her. He saw her next at a friend's dinner party, where she was clay in his hands, smooth and easily warmed. She didn't protest when he found a simple cot in a servant's quarters for his delicate advances. By then, he was an expert with the clothes. In the aftermath, she admitted it had been her first time, and he humbly pledged it would not be the last.

Another week later, he learned why she hadn't answered his letters. Ever so tactfully, Bronte informed him Simone had moved up her wedding date with the Vicomte de Brignala. Bronte tried to console Athos, but he refused the pity or the enticement of more women and parties. After a sullen weekend alone in his bedroom, Athos made his friend take him home. Next time, Athos had promised himself, he would be more careful.

Athos chose lovers with singular devotion. Like sword-play, a relationship with a woman demanded focus, and he savoured being true to one woman for long stretches. It was more satisfying. More intense. Without question, he loved women. They occupied many of his thoughts and underscored too many of his motives. But he did *not* love superficiality. He wanted his lovers to be his and his alone. He wanted their commitment because his soul needed equal care. He almost obtained his idealistic goal once or twice, but inevitably the affairs ended for one reason or another. His reserve of hope, to find "the one," was lower than ever.

But he was not giving up, not with Anne in his sights.

•     •     •

He intended to use the library as the starting point. He prized it above most other places. He spent more time in it than any other room in the estate, except his bedroom, where he allowed no one, including Bronte. Besides hunting and fencing and new political duties as provincial head, reading filled his life. If Anne loved books as he did, the library would deliver love potion to her heart.

In square footage, it was the largest room at Valliere, which was adequate in size for a château but by no means the biggest or most luxurious in the central provinces. By all accounts, it was an elegant, refined country villa ornamented with iron cresting and lunettes. But compared to the Castle of Bragelonne, the closest château, Valliere was a cottage. Nevertheless, it was well-appointed by his father, who took an interest in fine furniture and art. Only small vestiges of his mother still survived, a tapestry, an embroidered pillow or two. She died after a brief illness before he had formed many memories of her.

The books were literary, theological, philosophical, and even erotic. He and Bronte had discovered the books of flesh in their pre-adolescence. One, a "pillow book" from the Orient, contained lush coloured-ink drawings of porcelain-skinned women and men in seductive and imaginative sexual acts. Each picture was a double-page image of exquisite realism that caused Athos to hold his breath. As a boy, the art motivated him to want to attempt every single position. By the time he was twenty, he had done most.

Athos had never shown the book to anyone but Bronte. He believed his father had wanted him to find it because it had materialised one day next to an adventure book that Athos had read to tatters. He had slipped the pillow book into a coat and stole it up the secret stair to his bedroom wing and kept it for several months. He had taken pains not to soil it.

In the hour before his guests' arrival, Athos wondered if he should rearrange the library chairs to make more intimate spaces. The furniture would impress Anne, of course, but he also wanted to create some privacy in case their attraction warranted it. The room was spacious, easy to get lost in. Near the grandiose window, he pushed two wingback chairs to touch at the armrests. He cast a third chair off into a corner. No need for company.

The door to the library swung open as he finished. Alone, Bronte appeared flush. "Well rested?"

"Not a wink. Where are our guests?" Athos looked over his shoulder into the hall.

"About our guests ..."

Suddenly, Margot and Genue came shuffling through the door and stopped short, eyes widening at the largest of the room.

"My word." Genue loosened the wrap from her neck.

Margot blinked, awestruck. "This is the largest library I've ever seen."

"Three-thousand books," Athos said. He was aiming for cordial but secretly wished they'd vanish. "Where's Anne?"

"Didn't Bronte tell you?" Genue pulled off her gloves. "She's not coming."

"I was just getting to that ..." Bronte started, but Athos was already out in the hall, checking in both directions. "Mademoiselles, if you'll excuse us for a moment."

Bronte followed Athos down the corridor. "Hold on."

"Where is she?" Athos stomped to the end of the hall.

"She said she couldn't come because of a prior engagement at church."

"It's the middle of the week and an afternoon. What could she possibly have to do?"

Bronte shook his head.

"Did she write a note?" Athos asked.

"Nothing. I didn't see her. I didn't find out she wasn't coming until I picked up the other two."

Shrieks of laughter peeled into the hallway from the library.

"You first." Bronte waved back in the direction of the chamber.

Genue and Margot sat hunched over a book on the velvet chaise. Had they been sitting any closer, they would have been in each others' laps. Margot glanced up as Athos approached, the blush in her cheeks as rosy as a summer sunset.

"This is positively scandalous." Her hand covered up an image in the Oriental pillow book.

"Where on Earth did you get this?" Genue never lifted

her gaze from the page.

*How did they find this one?*

Bronte smirked and winked at Athos, whose good humor had disappeared.

"That was my father's," he said and slipped it from their laps, though not before Genue turned back a few pages.

"That one is my favourite," she said, pointing and craning her neck at one of the few positions Athos hadn't indulged, a *ménage a trois*.

"Mademoiselles." He nodded once, slapped the book shut and dropped it into a nearby desk drawer.

"Oh, I almost forgot." Margot lifted a bottle of wine from her bag on the floor. "This is from Anne."

"Did she relay a message with it?" Athos took the bottle to the desk, inspecting the shape and the colour of its contents. The top of the cork was stamped with a tulip.

"She said it wasn't for us to drink. It was only for you."

The men exchanged glances.

"And what do you suggest we do now?" Bronte asked. Both women glared at the desk drawer. "Besides that."

Athos used every ounce of patience throughout the afternoon. He distracted the women from their prurient notions with ordinary picture books of landscapes and art from India and Italy. When they became excitable again by the nudes in a book of Greek sketches, he decided to take them outside to the garden. He needed air.

He let the women walk ahead along the flower beds.

"I guess this is for the best." Athos wondered if Bronte missed Demi, too. "This is a sign that I should speak to Father de Breuil."

"I wouldn't call it an outright rejection. She did send the wine."

"What do you think she's up to?"

"Nothing; no different than any woman," Bronte said. "She's playing hard to get."

"After the other day? She nearly ate me alive with her eyes."

"Or was it the other way around?" Bronte picked a tall daisy and slowed down. "Look, she's gorgeous, like I told you, and obviously she's navigated the waters with men before. The way I see it, you have the advantage. Privilege, wealth, and the freedom to play the game. Much more freedom than she has, in fact. Go see her brother if you're still interested."

"You sound like you don't care one way or the other. A few days ago, you were bargaining to make me see her and arguing to spare the formalities. Namely, her virtue."

"I just know you, Athos. In any case, promise me you won't closet yourself off in your room for the next week, licking your wounds. She did send the wine. Just for you." Bronte's eyes brightened again with possibilities.

Athos nodded to the other guests. "I can't spend any more time with these two. Can you?"

Bronte obliged. Athos said his good-byes and sent the party to his pond with a basketful of pâte and sparkling wine.

After dusk, he returned to the library to contemplate his next move and to slowly drink his way to the bottom of her wine. It was gritty with sediment. As for taste, it ranked low on his palate. After an hour, his head drooped from side to side, so he laid on the velvet lounge to sleep it off.

Though heavy in the chest, he felt afloat. The light from a candle cast strange shadows. A few shapes turned into figures drifting in and out of his blurry mind. *A servant? A ghost?* The dark silhouettes moved like fluid in his grogginess. Whispers swirled in the grey-black. Voices hissed around him. Fragments of sentences bounced from the walls and inside his head.

He heard his name. *Fere. Fere. So young. So beautiful.*

The murmurs circled like smoke. His cheeks grew hot, and his head tossed heavily. Cool air washed over his body, and his clothes fluttered. Fingers like butterfly wings passed over his chest, bare to the waist. His body tensed, and the fine hairs on his middle bristled with warmth. The feeling, the breath or the wind, teased past his navel and lower. His most sensitive skin awoke. A familiar tingle grew between his legs until his loins ached. The waves of sensation became a rush, and he arched and held on, toward the final pitch, suspended in pleasurable warmth for the lightning. It ran down him in a shudder so superb, he awoke at its strike.

He sat up with a start, sweaty and temples throbbing. It was soft black in the library. Athos found his shirt unbuttoned and trousers undone. A blanket covered his lower legs. He brought it up over the rest of his body and struggled to fall back asleep. He went over and over the details of the dream. *Was it a dream? Who had spoken? Given him a blanket?* His servants weren't known to be so attentive, and asking would just invite strange stares.

His headache worsened, and he drank a pitcher of water left at the desk. He sniffed the wine bottle, but it didn't smell foul. He checked the doors to the hall and to the secret passageway to his private wing and locked them. He followed the cool air from a library window left ajar. Closing it, he determined he must talk to Anne's brother tomorrow. He wanted to arrange to meet her on proper terms, and he wanted information, everything good and not so good, as much as he could persuade the priest to tell him about Anne.

# 4

# The Ways of Women

Athos wore his finest doublet and shaved in preparation for his visit to Father de Breuil. While polishing his boots, a servant knocked on his bedroom door and announced from the hall that a woman was waiting for him in the library.

"Demi!" Athos grabbed her hands and kissed them before bringing her to the armchairs he'd rearranged for Anne. "It's been too long."

"I'm sorry to come by unannounced." She looked around the room and to the door. "Are you alone?"

The way she asked reminded him why he found her so appealing. She was like a fawn, timid and earthy. Athos often wondered how Bronte had convinced her to love him.

"You're always welcome. Bronte said you were ill."

"Not quite." She removed her gloves and stuffed them in the seat cushions. "That was the only excuse I could think of to get out of yesterday's visit. That's one reason I'm here, to apologise for my absence."

"You're not sick?"

"Not even a sniffle. I just—I try to limit my time with Margot and Genue."

"Hmm." Even good girls lied, and in this case, he understood why Demi might fib to spare herself the company. "They *do* push the boundaries of good taste."

"They make me uncomfortable. I'm ashamed of lying, but my sensibilities don't fit theirs. Please forgive me."

"No, no, it's fine." He patted her knee and was about to describe yesterday's events when the wrinkle across her forehead deepened. "What's wrong? Not Margot and Genue?"

"It's Bronte. Have you seen him recently?" She was wringing a handkerchief that she had pulled from a sleeve.

"He was here most of the afternoon. He entertained while I sulked. The party was missing the honoured guest. Do you know her? The new priest's sister?"

"I've heard about her from Margot and Genue, but I haven't met her. Did Bronte seem preoccupied yesterday?"

"Not at all. He was as dutiful to my usual mood swings as ever." His joke made her smile less than usual. "Whatever is bothering you must be serious. When my self-loathing doesn't make you laugh, it's a sign of trouble."

"I think I'm losing him." She stared out the grandiose window.

"That's impossible."

"We haven't been together in several weeks."

Demi had never been so candid. To Bronte's credit, he was a gentleman about their affair, keeping the specifics of their intimacies a secret.

"Are you certain you want to share this with me? Bronte keeps your intimate life close to his heart, even from the likes of me."

"That's exactly it. He doesn't say anything because we have not been intimate. He's very good at maintaining pretences."

Athos stopped himself from blurting, *What?* Nevertheless, the surprise felt like a punch in the chest, where his hand came to rest. "You and Bronte have not ... been together?"

"No. Never. And in the last few weeks, I haven't seen him once. He hasn't come to visit me or made any attempt to communicate."

"But he said you were sick. I thought he had seen you."

"I told Margot to tell him. He never came to check on me."

Athos went to a side window and swung it open. The cool air helped him think. When he returned to her, Demi's eyes glistened with hurt. His heart ached in return.

Athos knelt and hugged her shoulders. "Oh, Demi. You'll have to excuse my shock, but I was always under the assumption that you and he had been one."

"I know. He wanted everyone to think that, and we've come close several times. But I had decided to wait. It's a gift for the day we marry."

"Such a beautiful gift, and also, sadly complicated." Athos squeezed her hands and sat back down. "I guess you must question whether its causing his distance."

"After two years, who wouldn't?"

Athos sympathised; remaining chaste posed more problems for women. "I admire your decision. You have a true heart. Don't doubt yourself."

She stood abruptly and started pacing. "He's been growing distant since last fall, the weeks you two were in Paris." She pinched the bridge of her nose. "I actually encouraged him to take you. All of us were concerned for your well-being. It seemed like the best thing he could do to bring you out of mourning."

"Ironically, it did, and it didn't. It stopped the immediate pain, yes." *The women, the parties, what man wouldn't be spoiled?* But it had also confirmed his emptiness. "I didn't succeed in finding what Bronte has with you. You're still his one." The last words stuck in his throat.

"After he came back, he talked less frequently about our future. At first, I thought he was still concerned about you, but then I began to see it much differently."

"How so?"

"He was jealous." She stopped pacing, like a rabbit caught in the crosshairs of an archer.

Athos screwed his face into uncertainty. "Of me?"

"You were free to take up with anyone. Everyone. Paris loved you. You were the new provincial prince full of handsome confidence. He was just your escort, a servant to your whims."

"But he took part in all of it. He made all the connections and the liaisons." And participated in all the pleasures, too, but Athos didn't want to say more.

"I'm not naïve, Athos. I know he probably slept with many women while he was there. I don't blame him for it.

He's a man." She held his stare for several seconds. "He probably even had more women than you."

Athos never had cause to believe Demi's devotion to Bronte wavered, until now. Because of the way she said *you*. *You*, meaning the better man. A small tinder hung in the air between them.

Whether or not her observation was laden with other feelings, he couldn't argue. Bronte was as smooth as oiled silk when it came to convincing women to share themselves with him. While in Paris, Athos had to stop nagging Bronte about the damage it might do to his soul and his relationship with Demi. The debauchery was a subject only Bronte could reconcile with God, and Athos was too busy wallowing in self pity to keep after him.

A little shaken, Athos took Demi's hand and guided her to sit. "Are you sure he's avoiding you? Maybe he's just busy. I've asked him to help me find out more about Anne. Maybe I should do that myself." He forced a small laugh, but it came out flatly.

"He's not busy. He's withdrawn, at least from me."

"I'll talk to him," Athos assured, petting her hand. "Let me see what he's thinking."

"Please don't tell him what I've confided. It would crush him."

He smiled, trying to convey normalcy. "No wonder you and I are his closest friends."

"Why?"

"We take religion seriously," he said, and she started to laugh at him, but he placed a finger near her lips to shush her. Being close to her made him happy. "I do take it seriously, you know. I hope to win over the priest's sister as honourably as I can. No sins of the flesh. Not this time."

"If she's half as beautiful as I've heard, it will require more willpower than you needed during your two months in Paris."

She finally smiled back at him. He promised to send word once he spoke to Bronte. Before Demi departed, he loaned her several books about gardening.

•　　•　　•

On the ride to the village church in Averdon, Athos couldn't get Demi's visit out of his head. Her anxiety was similar to his own. Their hearts were, too. They believed love was a bounty—a source of wholeness. But the sweetest part—the sensuality—was forbidden. The apple of knowledge in the Garden of Eden. Athos had reached for it many times in the past and had grown accustomed to its taste. He had taken the fruit for granted, despite the damage to his soul.

Among his friends, he could not think of any bachelors who were saving themselves for marriage. His first experience with a woman, a girl, happened when he was sixteen, a wild and clumsy tumble with a sheep farmer's daughter. She was sent away before he could practice again. His friends and father shamelessly, though secretly, celebrated his conquest, while she was punished and banished to a convent.

Demi's disclosure confounded him. He would have bet his estate that she and Bronte had been lovers. Discrete, certainly, but lovers nonetheless. In one way, it saddened him that they had not yet shared their deepest selves with one another. Although sex was a sin out of wedlock, making love with a treasured partner, such as Demi was to Bronte, meant paradise. Lust was one thing, memorable and irresistible, but sex with a true love was mutual oblivion. In a perfect world, he would find it.

Athos arrived at the church well before the hour of vespers. The large door creaked for lack of oil. Very few candles burned inside, typical because the church mainly served a community of farmers. Everyone would be in the fields. Athos walked down the centre of the pews, not knowing what to anticipate from Father de Breuil.

His sermon Sunday about Genesis never veered into unfamiliar territory. The book was one of Athos's favourites. To him, the story of Genesis was significant in that God developed everlasting forgiveness. He created the world, destroyed it in a flood, started over, and pledged never to wipe it out again. God's regret made him a tolerant God, at least for man's imperfections.

The other joy that Genesis gave Athos was Adam's reaction to Eve.

*You are bone of my bone. Flesh of my flesh.*

Athos believed it was the first love poetry ever uttered.

*We are one*, Adam was saying, naked in the garden, next to his one love. *You are mine.*

The silence of the sanctuary made Athos pause. He listened to his breathing and inhaled incense and exhaled potential. Heading toward the priest's study, a cold chill blew from the direction of the confessionals. He strained and heard a door click shut. Aware it might be the priest, he walked over and found the hem of a silvery fabric protruding from a closed confessional door. Someone rustled inside.

He stepped up to the door, but the priest's booth was empty. A voice from within the next compartment stopped him from knocking.

"Delays, delays." Followed by a long sigh.

Athos froze. It was Anne.

She started humming, a nocturne or a hymn. It was lovely, the pitch and the drama, like she was purring the notes in secret contentment. The hum deepened. He knew if he made any sound he would give himself away, and part of him wanted to. The other part was fascinated by the cat in the cupboard.

A minute passed and the notes from her lengthened until she wasn't singing. Her tone imparted animalistic pleasure, the kind from a cat of bigger size. He'd hear an *mmm* and an *umh* while the fabric of her dress shifted inside the cramped, wooden box. Her hands were making long passes across the fabric—*Where would that place them now?* Her breath hitched and resumed, heavy with need. The movement sounded like swirls of an autumn breeze, fanning her body. Dramatic rests interspersed her music. She was holding her breath. Longer and longer. The fabric rubbed in rhythm. He nearly spoke, taking the words right out of her mouth, his own lips pressed moistly to the door, at the moment she peaked: *Oh God.* The air rushed out of her, and the stray hem of the skirt slipped inside at the vibration.

All the wind left him, too, though under tight control. He laid his palms silently on either side of the door and dropped his head. *Air, I need air.* He tried to collect himself and move. His body was rigid. All that separated her from him was a slat of wood and a metal swivel. In every other way, they were on the same plateau.

"Excuse me." The voice hit him from behind like a splash

of frigid water. Athos buckled and straightened as quickly. Father de Breuil stood at the centre of the pews, leaving several rows between them. "May I help you?"

Athos met him as far from the confessional as his body could accommodate. "Father, my apologies. I didn't intend to come by unannounced."

"This is a house of God. Our doors are open at any time. How may I help you, my son?"

Athos offered a handshake and walked them away from the cat. "I am Comte de la Fere, the sovereign of Berry. I've wanted to meet you since your arrival last month."

Father de Breuil had the look of a priest down to the last detail: flawless posture, empathetic eyes, and a straight jaw. Athos thought it was almost too perfect.

"The sovereign? You look familiar," the priest said. "Do I know you from somewhere?"

"Here. I attended last Sunday's Mass. You spoke from Genesis."

"Of course." The priest's brow relaxed. "Though most of what I remember is that you caused a bit of an uproar in my flock because of your surprise visit."

"It was completely unintended."

"The sovereign, you say? I've never met a sovereign who looks so ..."

"So young?" Athos's jaw clenched a fraction, but he eked out a smile. "My father passed away just over a year ago."

"I'm sorry to hear that. Please accept my sympathy. And forgive my forwardness, but does your father have anything to do with your visit today?" The priest glanced to the confessional, which was as still as a grave.

"No, nothing like that." Athos resumed their stroll, keeping one ear out for the cat. "I'm here because of your sister."

The priest nearly reversed course. "Anne isn't here right now."

The priest's expression seemed over-protective and curious. Still, the poor light hindered a better read, and Athos grew anxious that either he, or she, would be discovered. He motioned for the door.

"Anne is the friend of one of your parishioners, Margot." Athos arrived several yards from the door. "She's the cousin of my dear friend Demi. But my friend and Margot are on poor terms." Not a lie, he rationalised. "I was wondering if it might be possible for Anne to picnic with them at my estate? It might soften the awkwardness between them if they had someone else to interact with. And, it would give Demi and I the chance to meet Anne."

"Are the women quarrelling?"

"Let's just say Margot and Demi don't see eye to eye."

"I'm not sure Anne would be any help in your cause. She's got a strong sense of herself and her opinions. And her social calendar is filling up quickly. A man was here just yesterday from Berry who occupied her most of the afternoon."

"I probably know whom."

"To be quite honest with you, I thought he was the sovereign." The priest chuckled.

A thud came from the direction of the confessional. Athos might have pursued the conversation further, but his nerves got the best of him. He didn't want Anne spilling out to find him huddled with her brother, who had just seen Athos at the door to her hiding place.

"Please, at least give Anne my invitation," Athos said, moving right in front of the exit. "The picnic is Saturday."

The priest nodded, and after an abbreviated bow, Athos was breathing fresh air again.

# Coincidences

A servant announced Athos's arrival at the mansion of Bronte's family in Blois and brought two swords outside to the inner courtyard, a routine occurrence.

"It's time for a talk and a round," Athos told Bronte as he waved him outside. Their polished swords gleamed in the sun.

By far, Athos was the better swordsman. He had worked with many teachers over the years and lately was paying one to travel from Poitiers each month to Valliere. As for sparring partners, Bronte was a challenge because of his tendency to set aside all the rules and launch into wild attacks, unsportsmanlike but with a dash of good humour. Though playful, their games always carried a competitive undercurrent.

They smiled, bowed and squared off. Their routine was a finely tuned clock.

"*Engarde.*" Athos shuffled to one side awaiting Bronte's usual first attack. "I just came from my scouting trip to the new priest."

Bronte slammed twice on the right, and the swords clanged. "And did you see Anne?"

"On the contrary." Athos attacked with a double feint that caused Bronte to momentarily lose his balance. Bronte's eyes narrowed.

"If you didn't, then why are you here?" Sweat already glistened Bronte's brow.

"She was hiding in the confessional. I don't think she knew I was there. But I certainly got an earful."

"Of a confession?"

"Not exactly." Athos flicked his blade in a deft, underhanded swipe. Bronte usually protested because Athos used the move to show off skills that only a master could execute. "She was—how can I put it delicately—taking liberties with herself while locked inside the booth."

Bronte let down his guard. "She was ..." With his free hand, he made a circular motion between his legs.

Athos nodded and blew a kiss to Heaven. "She purred like a mountain lion."

"I can't believe it!" Bronte whirled around and cut across the air. "Where were you? In the priest's booth?"

"It was sacrilegious enough to be outside her door. She doesn't suspect I overheard. At least, I don't think she does."

The spark in Bronte's eyes became a fire, the likes of a man possessed by a burning vision he had no chance of touching. "You're wicked," he finally said. A sinister smile showed his daydream had raced to new heights. "Did you enjoy it?"

"You have to ask?" Athos pinched his blade and ran his fingers down the length of it. "And I don't believe I'm the wicked one. She's much more fiery than I'd imagined."

"How could you tell what she was doing?" The question was half in jest.

"You're two years my senior and many more notches ahead of me in lovers." Athos wrapped an arm around Bronte's shoulder. "How many of yours reach the pinnacle in complete silence? At her release, she rattled the entire enclosure and evoked God."

"Then you did enjoy it," Bronte said, slipping from under his arm.

"*She* certainly did. Then the priest caught me."

Bronte's howl of amusement caused a few birds to flutter off the mansion roof. "He caught you listening?"

"He thought I wanted to confess. He had no idea she was there, but I quickly distracted him from my entertainment." Athos twirled his sword. "I asked him to invite her to the château for a picnic. I'm hopeful she'll attend this time. What insight do you have? The priest said a man from Berry visited her yesterday. I assumed that was you."

"Anne and I spoke briefly." Bronte started for the entrance gate but came around after Athos tapped his shoulder with the blade.

"And?" Athos took the ready position.

Bronte shrugged. "It's as you say. She's not like other women."

"Obviously. Did you speak of me?"

"I asked her if she might accept an invitation to Berry again."

"Yes?"

"She wanted us to know that she and her friends like to go to Agape Lake on very hot days. She said if you want to see her again, to come the day the sun is full and high."

Athos dropped his sword. "But she won't come to Valliere?"

"It's not as if she said no. She's as wily as a snake."

"You sound frustrated."

Bronte knocked blades with a force that made Athos's hand hurt. "I think she knows how to play men, and if you want her, you should take her."

"You know my answer to that this time." Athos stood *engarde* again.

Bronte mirrored it. "And that's your weakness."

"I want her on my own terms."

"Your terms are like your swordsmanship—they lack ruthlessness." Bronte surged on Athos, attempting two, then three attacks.

Athos retreated and riposted. "But I'm the better swordsman."

"In a real fight, high-mindedness gets you nowhere." Bronte lunged with jab after jab. "Your goodness will always be your weakness. To win, you must know pain." With his forearm, Bronte pinned Athos to an awning post. "Only pain makes you ruthless. Your privilege protects you from it. So far." He snarled and backed off.

Athos felt the blood rush from his face. "I'll be rewarded. Wait and see." He smoothed his shirt straight. "But *you* wait too long. Why haven't you asked Demi to marry you yet?"

"How do you know that?"

"Because I've asked you nearly every day since you said you would."

Bronte stirred up dirt with his foot and kicked the dust. "What's the hurry? She's waiting for me whether I marry her now or next year."

Athos grabbed Bronte's hand on the pommel. "What's wrong with you? She's your true love. She's good and meek and faithful, a fine complement to your nature. You'll not find it with any other woman, and you could start a family, have an heir."

"Heirs are pointless if there's no title to hand down."

"Your logic burns me. A son is the prize of love and marriage. You'll make your fortune soon with your father's guidance. I can help, too, if you'd let me."

"Yes, yes, all of that." Bronte fluttered his hand in front of him as if handing out favours. "Tokens and plans and hard work," Bronte marched toward a water trough. "I have principles, too, you know. If I buy any rank, it'll be from my own labour."

"You have the world at your fingertips, if you'd just ask for it," Athos said, trying not to talk down, "yet you act like a child whose pony ran off."

Bronte splashed water on his face. Annoyed, Athos grabbed his wrist, but Bronte struggled free. "No, Athos. It's you who has the world laid before him. Wealth, privilege, women. You're blind to the spoils."

"But you have them, too. In Paris, we were unstoppable."

Bronte lapsed into a blank stare. "The way they looked at you. Do you recall? Everyone was astounded by your youthful charisma. They loved you without knowing you. You didn't have to prove a thing."

Athos shook Bronte's shoulder. "And what good is false admiration? Their fascination was shallow. There's not a single person in Paris that I would trade our friendship for. No one came close, especially the women." Athos offered a handshake. "Take your rightful place among men. Our old exploits are ours to treasure, but we're getting older. Let's move forward. You're lucky to have someone like Demi to move forward with."

"I should be the one giving out the advice." Bronte slumped on the edge of the trough. "A proposal is delicate, and you seem much more romantic than me. How should I do it?"

Athos slapped his friend on the back, grinned, and walked them out of the innyard. It was a rare moment that he did not relish a well-planned strategy.

•　•　•

The heat arrived and, so too, the day for the proposal. He and Bronte dallied on the ride to Agape Lake to give Demi time to reach their berry-picking destination first. They counted on Anne being there, a planned coincidence.

Agape Lake was one of the most gorgeous spots in the entire province. The trees made pockets of privacy beside sparkling views of the water. Waterfowl, small songbirds, and an occasional crane delighted seekers of its sanctuary. Lovers were rumoured to cavort in the leafy shadows of the many trees and flora.

"Have you practised what you'll say?" Athos asked of Bronte, who was letting his horse graze by the lake road a little too long.

"How about, 'Marry me'?"

"You're struggling."

"Then enlighten me," Bronte said, flipping his hand above his head. "What would one of your poets say?"

"You wouldn't deliver a poem seriously, I'm afraid. Your own words will sound more sincere."

"What's the use of getting flowery?" Bronte said. "I love her. She loves me. She'll say yes. The end."

Athos galloped ahead instead of grinding the subject. Close to the lake under a large oak, he found shade for the horses and limbs to hang their coats and hats. The heat was making the air wavy on the horizon. By the time they walked to an outcrop of raspberry bushes about one hundred rods from the bank, they had worked up a sweat.

Athos heard voices near the water's edge and the sound of someone running, perhaps a child. He didn't have a chance to check before Demi hurtled through a break in the foliage. She was breathing heavily, and her face was flush. She looked back and forth from Athos to Bronte several times, unable to catch her breath. Then she stepped up to Bronte, face to face.

"Is this why you wanted me here? To act like them?" She slapped Bronte's cheek abruptly, and he stumbled backward, wide-eyed and bleeding from a split lip. She gasped and covered her own mouth.

"Demi, what's the matter?" Athos moved toward her, but she suddenly looked ashamed and ran toward the woods. From Bronte's shrug, Athos could tell that an important piece of information had been held back. Bronte wiped the blood from his lip and headed after her.

Motionless, Athos listened to the sounds of laughter and frolicking by the lake, a backdrop that made Demi's actions seem much more bizarre. He couldn't recall seeing her so rattled or angry. Whatever "them" was doing didn't suit her in the least.

Moving closer to the bank, Athos aimed for a thicket of tall bushes, beyond which the voices and splashes grew louder. Out of sight, he could hear Anne, Genue and Margot playing in the water—more specifically, shrieking in good humour. The sky was bright white, and the sounds of the merriment bounced off the water in shrill tones.

As Athos pushed aside the thick greenery, the light flashing off the water blinded him. All he could do was squint. He blinked several times, until his sight was dazzled by more scorching images. The women lolled about in the water as naked as nymphs. Their skin radiated like sprays of Queen Anne's lace.

He immediately crouched down, broke his gaze, and took several gulps of air. He clutched his throat and felt his pulse race ahead of him. If he backtracked for Demi, he might interrupt Bronte's proposal—or apology—but Athos didn't feel like running. Instead of blatantly watch, he closed his eyes and listened.

He recognised Anne's voice right away. "Do you suppose she'll come back?"

"Don't worry about my cousin," Margot said. The water splashed. "She may never join us, but maybe seeing us will loosen her up."

Anne laughed. "Bronte thought so. She has a lot to learn if she's never been with anyone before. He might be a little disappointed."

Margot giggled. "Don't blame her, Anne. She's saving herself."

Anne affected a thick French accent. "*My tongue, Madame, would eagerly express; Lord, I cannot look less than loathingly.*"

Athos recognised the line from the du Bellay poem in an instant. He squeezed his eyes tighter.

"I don't understand any of that poetry you spout off. What's the point? A lover wants only one thing from your tongue," Genue said.

"Words are the most powerful tool you have," Anne answered. "Not only can they arouse the flesh, you can also use them to seduce your lover's mind. It's more important than any curve you possess because a poem can win a man's soul."

"Oh, you think you know so much." Margot sounded condescending. "A kiss is a kiss, is a kiss, is a kiss. There's nothing that'll make it more than it is."

"Come here, and I'll teach you, if you're brave enough."

Athos heard shallow splashes near the bank toward Anne's voice. He broke into a profuse sweat, battling his scruples. Wasn't it every boy's dream to secretly watch a naked woman without her knowing? His entire life, the opportunity to peep had never arisen. Now three women? Their conversation alone was sinful, and the stakes had just been raised. How would he explain *this* to Father Turre? Praying for forgiveness, he crossed himself and opened his eyes.

Standing in the lake up to mid-calf, the three women could have been statues of ivory painted pink in all the right places—their lips, their nipples, and yes, the quaint cherubs between their legs.

Anne was the most relaxed with herself. In charge. Her beauty surpassed the others. Her breasts were plump and firm, and the hair between her legs was a sandy tulle. Her body was a prime thoroughbred, taut and muscular in a satiny way. As Margot approached her, Anne's breaths came more rapidly, causing droplets beneath her bosom to glide past her belly button.

Athos would have given away his finest swords and horses to taste the water trickling down her skin.

As soon as Margot stood near, Anne began to trace the outline of Margot's breast. Margot shied at first but relaxed when Anne shushed her. She said nothing else but continued to make passes around Margot's breast until the nipple was tight with excitement. For her next act, Anne laid a cheek on Margot's collarbone.

"Now Margot, a lover's touch is exciting, as I've demonstrated. But if I speak my heart while I enjoy your body, you'll find there's a difference." Anne continued to tickle Margot's breast while reciting. "*Drink with me, play with me, love with me, be wreathed with me; be wild when I am wild; and when I am still, be still.*"

Margot shuddered as Anne kissed her cleavage and ran a hand up the small of her back. It came to rest just in time to catch Margot.

In exquisite pain, Athos curled up and moaned as low as he could. His heart rumbled and body rang. He felt dangerously out of control. The good and bad of what he had just seen sullied his moral base. Anne was an angel and a demon. Eternal dark and first light.

As Athos rallied for composure, Bronte materialised.

"Did you see that?" Athos asked, hoping he hadn't.

"See what?"

"That," he said and pointed toward the lake.

Bronte bent down to peer through the brush. "You're quite daring to get so close." He slapped Athos's shoulder in congratulations.

Then the pieces fell together. "You knew they were going to be swimming today—in the nude," Athos said. "Why did you think bringing Demi out here was a good idea? That was irresponsible and smells a little like sabotage. Did you talk to her?"

"She's furious. She blames me, of course. I thought, maybe, just maybe ..." Bronte kept staring through the looking glass of grass.

"You thought she would join them?" Athos began crawling from the lookout spot and tugged the cuff of Bronte's pants for him to follow. He kicked at Athos instead. Furious, Athos struggled to keep his voice down. "Don't you know anything about Demi by now?"

Bronte hissed back at him. "What's that supposed to mean? That I'm insensitive? That I'm the only one to blame here?"

"Those women know more about your relationship with Demi than you've cared to share with me."

"So."

"I overheard Anne saying you planned this. Did you? With her? Is that what you talked about with Anne the other day?"

"It's Margot who knows everything about everyone, including Demi." Bronte took one last look through the parted greenery. "They've gossiped themselves into a beautiful state of titillation, don't you think?"

"Why did you allow this to happen?" Athos's head throbbed. "Why would you want Demi to be somewhere where she doesn't belong?"

Nostrils flaring, Bronte finally started crawling toward Athos. "Because I'm tired of waiting, Saint Athos. Because I want Demi, and she's not mine."

"But she is yours. Why can't you see that?"

"She's not mine like I want her to be. Not like I've longed for her, ached for her, not like ... like ..."

"Like Anne."

Bronte was standing now, and his eyes had softened. His body looked limp in the joints. His hands went to his heart. Athos soon discovered the reason.

Behind him, Anne stood at the tree where their coats hung, draping her dress over the front of her wet body. The contour of her hip and leg peeked out from behind the inadequate cover. She didn't seem to care in the least.

She drew a circle in the dirt with her toe. "Did you ask for me?"

Athos bolted upright next to Bronte, and both cleared their throats. Out of respect, Athos instinctively turned his back, though it felt absurd. He jerked Bronte around, too, which required several insistent punches. Bronte, still red from their argument, shot him a searing look: *Are you insane?*

"I think Bronte has the right idea," Anne said, her voice as warm as fresh milk.

Athos pinched the bridge of his nose and recovered his dignity. "Mademoiselle, you are undeniably beautiful." His throat tightened. "But I don't know you, and I'm obliged to look the other way when a woman is compromised."

"Your conduct seems odds," she said. "Weren't you staring through the bushes?"

Athos could not cover up the obvious place where the ground and grass had been disturbed. Bronte hitched up an eyebrow in an *I-told-you-so* way.

"Please accept my apologies." Athos truly meant it. "Demi came running from your direction very upset. Bronte had no part in my investigation. He went to check on her."

This time, Bronte tipped his head in thanks.

Anne's dress crinkled behind them. "I invited you here. There's no need to apologise. Does our bathing shock you? I can't image it does completely."

"Our acquaintance is just beginning, Mademoiselle."

"Call me Anne, please, and I shall call you Fere."

"Of course. Anne, I would much prefer we start our friendship fully dressed."

"Hmm. You are dressed." She walked closer. "But you watched us. What did you see?"

Athos swallowed back his desire to turn around. "I heard that you have an ear for poetry. I hope you'll share it with me in a more appropriate setting."

"Perhaps. Bronte, what do you think?"

Athos anxiously looked at him.

"Athos is my oldest friend, and sometimes he's too good for the world's low standards." Bronte pivoted and started toward her.

"Bronte—" Athos's admonishment was pointless the second it was spoken.

"Wait, Bronte has something to say," Anne said.

Athos glimpsed back, trying to focus on his friend and not on the temptress now between them.

"I think," Bronte said, beaming at her bare backside, "that you'll find each other impossible to resist." His eyes raced up her back, then closed as if he had eaten the most mouth-watering cake. "Enjoy it while it lasts." He slowly left them, and the air sparked in the silence.

She was no more than a few feet away, and Athos tracked the half-covered outline of her body to a black band on her upper arm. She didn't blush when he returned her sly smile, and Athos, fighting nature, turned away again.

"Why didn't you accept my first invitation to Valliere?" he asked.

Her skirt rustled again. "Did you enjoy my wine?"

"It was ... memorable." The memory and the heat made him light-headed.

"Were you arguing with Bronte?"

"No more than usual. We give each other great latitude."

"Bronte and you are very close, but you're also very different."

"He's always been the risk-taker," Athos said. "Our bond is deeper than blood."

"There's no jealousy between you and him?"

"I'd sacrifice my life for him." Even if Bronte felt jealous of him, it didn't seem to matter in their history together and was certainly not worth mentioning. "Please, Mademoiselle."

"Anne."

"Anne, please, at the risk of sounding parochial, please dress so I may face you."

"I will." But no noise indicated she did. "I'll come to Valliere tomorrow in my finest silks. To see if you are good."

"What do you mean, *good*?" He raised up his arms to reinforce he was doing his best.

"To see if we are a good match."

"And if we are?" His blood rushed to every natural spot.

"Then I must know if you're giving."

"And if so?"

"Then I shall see if you're game."

"Anne, I'm never the game. I'm always the prey." A dramatic silence followed. He'd finally slipped into her wicked trap. *God help me, my honour will be lost before I ever get to know her.*

A warm hand touched his neck. "Thank you," she said.

"For what?" He dropped his chin to his chest to expose more nape for her to touch. She did.

"Resisting."

As soon as she departed, he buckled to the ground and repeated several Hail Marys.

# The First Day

When Anne said silk, she meant silk. For the visit the next day to Valliere, Anne showed up in silk shoes, silk gloves, and a silk headband. A silk handkerchief dangled from her cuff. Athos was convinced silk wrapped her in many other places he couldn't see. She arrived an hour early for the picnic, well before Bronte.

To hold himself in check, Athos decided the library would be the safest place to take her. She circled the room in her beige gown, a confident swan, gliding in front of the grand window.

"Oh, Fere. The view's magnificent."

Athos reclined in one of the wingback chairs and stared at her. "Defies description."

On the contrary, he could easily describe her. Fair, very bright light blue eyes, black eyebrows and eyelashes, his equal in height and beautifully made. Her intangible qualities required a keener eye—an aura of self-confidence, a well-tuned sense of observation, and a sensuality that plunged a dagger through his heart.

"Do you come here often?" she asked, dragging a silken finger across a pane of glass. He was thankful he'd made the servants polish and dust every inch of the room the night before.

"There's only one other place here I spend more time."

"Your bedroom?" She peeked over her collar at him.

He disciplined his voice not to crack. "I'm more of a night person. I have a tendency to be up and down in the dark. I usually end up here." He nodded to the velvet chaise, his second bed.

She crossed over to it. As she sat, she swept her hand across the fabric and then her cheek. "I also love the night."

*How does she do it?* She'd been inside less than fifteen minutes and already he needed relief. He pointed himself to the bookshelves and selected a scientific volume on flora and fauna.

"Poetry?" she asked.

The book fell open to a diagram of a bee pollinating an orchid. He slapped it shut and returned it to the shelf. "No."

He hastily found a book of devotions.

"You're a faithful man, I see." She slipped up behind him and slid a hand under his elbow to turn up the book cover. Her chin rested on his shoulder. "*Introduction to the Devout Life* by de Sale," she read. "I've enjoyed it many times."

He ducked from her and leaned against the shelf. "That doesn't surprise me, your brother being a priest. But how do you know poetry so well? *Be still when I am still.* That's an obscure verse. And Greek."

Her fingers skimmed across the titles as she walked the length of the shelf away from him. The silk sizzled with every step.

"You obviously enjoy reading." She stopped like a compass point at his poetry section. Her homing abilities were uncanny. She pulled a book from the bland colours. "But he who reads poetry is usually more than a reader. He loves it."

He opted to stay quiet. Watching her was poetry in and of itself.

She opened the book and focused on a sentence. *"He took the golden cup,"* her voice, too, was silk, *"and forthwith looked at it in wonder."*

She had found his only book of ancient Greek verse.

"It reads *she*," he said. "*She* took the golden cup."

"Is my translation poor?"

"Oh no." He tried hiding his smile. "Completely fitting."

In the next second, the door closed with a *bam*, and Bronte stood clicking his heels in front of Anne. "Mademoiselle de Breuil." He took her hand and bowed with the deft speed of a dragonfly. "So glad you could come. But where are your companions?"

"In a separate carriage." She smiled at both men. "Will Demi be joining us?"

Bronte's grin tightened around the edges. "She's unable to visit today."

Athos hadn't heard the verdict yet of Bronte's mission to claim Demi's hand in marriage. Now, he assumed a poor outcome.

"We could reschedule," Athos offered.

"No, no. By all means, our afternoon should be carefree." Bronte sat hard in the second wingback chair, pushing it even closer to the identical one next to it. He proceeded to brood and fixate on the view outside. "Are you two getting to know each other?"

"Fere's a poet." Her head sideways, Anne continued to read spines on the shelves.

"You're getting ahead of me," Athos said, trying to imagine the plain books with new eyes.

"No she's not." Bronte burrowed into the chair. "You do write poetry. You just don't share it."

"You never expressed an interest." Athos sat by his friend, a bit relieved to have him as a buffer from temptation, even if he was a surly one. "I write, but only for myself."

"Then why write at all?" Bronte thumped his knee nervously and fidgeted in the seat.

"What's your muse?" Anne flipped through a second book and strolled to the window.

"I don't have one in particular."

"No?" Bronte's knee froze as he laid out two soft white strips on the armrest. It took Athos a moment—Demi's gloves.

Bronte's expression was a gathering storm. "No muse at all?" He snatched the gloves up and stuffed them into his pocket.

"It's not what you think," Athos said, lower than normal. He needn't have bothered, for Anne appeared to be lost in the book. The thunder rolling in the room was isolated to the space between him and Bronte.

Anne turned a page. "A muse sparks the ember of your passionate self."

"It causes you to do things you wouldn't do otherwise," Bronte said, unblinking.

Athos shook his head. "My muse is pure and personal."

Bronte shot up from the chair and stalked across the room. "No wonder you haven't shared your work before. Pure and personal means secret from the world, for no one else to see."

"That isn't true," Athos said, torn between stopping his friend or letting him leave.

Bronte slammed the library door, which finally got Anne's attention.

"Fere?" She sat in the empty armchair, a trace indifferent. "Why did Bronte leave?"

"A misunderstanding." Athos smelled honeysuckle and Bronte's lingering hatred. "I should probably go talk to him."

"Must you now? It's our first day together." She laid the book on her lap, removed her gloves, and slid them into the cushion.

Athos felt out-of-sorts. He didn't want to spoil the moment with her, now that she was shining attention on him. She reached for his hand, stroked it, and placed it on the book, the closest he'd been to a woman in months. "Wouldn't it be brilliant to divine the contents of a book by simply placing your hands on it?"

A silly thought, but nonetheless, he listened.

"And if you could divine a book, could you also divine a person?" She leaned over the armrests and brought his hand to her cheekbone. "What am I thinking?"

His wanted to be bold but careful. "You may already know."

She exhaled, bringing the tips of his fingers to her lips. "Fere, you're thinking, *be here with me.*" Her lips tickled his palm, jarring the last of his self-control. "But what else?"

He relented and drew closer. "Touch me."

Her breath moistened the rough centre of his hand. "Yes?"

"Kiss me." Chasing his pulse, he knelt in front of her and found her mouth willing. Bronte was right. It had been too long. The smell of her, the feel of her, the taste of her stripped him of will power. Her knees pressed into his lower half. Her kiss was a bloom of youthfulness. Silk billowed around him, and her legs began to part. He gently wedged between them until he was touching the seat cushion, and his hands rounded her waist and down her hips. The silk smoothed the way over her thighs, where he began to bunch the fabric above her knees. She gasped but not very convincingly. Several of his kisses reversed her shock to a smile, until within the soft folds of fabric, an object jabbed him above the belt. The book. He broke from her lips to toss it, and as she nipped his ear, he glanced at the spine.

*Stop. Stop!*

"Fere?" Anne's whisper warmed his neck.

The book was white hot in his hand. Instantly, he withdrew from her silks and laid the Bible back in her lap. "This was a gift from my father."

He nestled her knees back together, but she gripped his shoulder, locking him still. She placed her other hand on the Bible in her lap and spoke as sharply as cut glass.

"There's light between us today. Even God said the light was good."

"He also created darkness at the same time." Athos removed her hand from his shoulder and kissed the back of it. "I want to take our time. Savor the creation."

It was just as well. Margot and Genue arrived seconds later, and Athos discovered that juggling three strangers was easier than handling the one. On the way to the pond, Anne kept sneaking glances and sending him smiles. The delicacies his servants set out for the picnic by the water kept their mouths busy for a little while: goose liver pâte, boiled quail eggs, sugared dates, and the basics—wine, crusty bread, and butter.

Anne licked butter from a finger rather than eat it with bread. "Your butter's sweet."

"It's churned with honey," Athos said, averting his eyes toward the pond when he could.

"This isn't fair." Margot left her place on the broad wool blanket and meandered toward the water's edge.

"What's not fair?" Genue asked, smearing pâte on a chunk of bread.

"You two have each other." She glanced to Anne and Athos. "What are we supposed to do all day?"

"Anne said you and Bronte were at Agape Lake yesterday while we were bathing," Genue said, a tease in her voice.

Athos caught Anne in a half-smile before she turned her head away. "Bronte asked Demi on an outing to pick berries," he said. "Unfortunately, that didn't happen."

"Did you see us?" Genue placed the emphasis on *see*.

"Your secret's safe with me."

Margot began fanning her face with a grassy frond that she had torn from the bank. "My word, Monsieur Athos, tsk, tsk."

"Fere's good at keeping secrets," Anne said as she reclined on her elbows and slanted her eyes toward him. "Apparently, Demi was here the other day without Bronte's knowledge."

Athos's heart rose to his throat. *She had been paying attention in the library.* "Demi's my friend."

In a flash, Margot was back on the blanket with her head against Genue's, fused together into one devilish agent of gossip. Athos frowned at each in turn, ending with Anne.

"Demi's in love with Bronte, and Bronte's my dearest and oldest friend," Athos said and began wrapping the leftovers to return them to the picnic basket.

"Why was she here without Bronte?" Genue asked, almost in unison with Margot.

"Bronte may not be the only one with the propensity to stray," Anne said, wiping the buttery gloss from her lips with a linen napkin.

Athos, on the verge of a blush, clopped the clay cover on the butter dish. "Demi's heart is true."

"It's not Demi of whom I speak." Smiling, Anne handed him her napkin. The eyes of Margot and Genue, the devilish duo, darted from Anne to Athos. A smattering of raindrops made everyone blink.

"You have much to learn about me." Athos poured the rest of the bottle of wine into his cup, grateful for the well-timed rain. He drank the wine in one swallow, and the warmth in his centre flared like a warning. Athos wasn't upset with Anne. Instead, she was living up to the challenge he had expected from her.

The rain turned into heavy drops, which caused the gossipy pair to run chortling toward the château. Athos quickly packed up the picnic, covered the basket with the blanket, and found a tree to leave it under. He squinted through the shower to see Anne rolling up her sleeves and walking into the water. Her shoes and stockings sat on the bank.

"Anne, you'll ruin your fine silk." But he was glad she had stayed. "What are you doing?"

The flair of her dress was soaked inches above the hem. "How will I get to know you if you keep secrets from the likes of your best friend?" she asked.

At the water's edge, he fumbled for an answer. Two could play the same game. "And how will I get to know *you* if you use your tongue like a sword? Some men would be put off by your intellect and guile."

"But you aren't."

He shook his head, chin down. It was all he could do to disguise his lust for another kiss. "I want to know you, Anne. Will you share yourself with me? Show me who you are?"

"When we meet again." She raised her face to the steady rain, opened her mouth, and flattened her tongue.

He walked into the water and recalled his boyhood fantasies of mermaids. "Soon, I hope."

"And then will you read me your poetry?" she asked. "Reveal to me your muse?" Raindrops wound down her cleavage.

"*Here by the splashing current Pan's pipe will entrance your spellbound eyes.*"

"That's Plato," she said.

"And his words, my seraphim, shall have to do for now."

He closed the subject with a too-brief kiss and chased her back to shelter, his feet barely touching the ground.

•    •    •

After the mid-day storm dissipated, Athos found Bronte in Blois, pacing the inner courtyard at his family's mansion, two swords at the ready.

Bronte had dug a long deep line in the dirt with the tip of his sword. The hair on Athos's neck rose. "Here all afternoon, I gather?"

Bronte, head and clothes damp from rain, threw a sword into Athos's body. The impact sent needles through his hand and arm.

"We'd better talk first," Athos said calmly.

"*Engarde*." The slight tremor in Bronte's stance wasn't from fear.

"I won't fight you." Athos dropped the sword and showed the whites of his hands. "You've got the wrong impression. Demi—"

"Ah, Demi. Innocent angel Demi." Bronte zig-zagged his sword between them as if marking the points across Athos's body that he planned to attack. "She didn't need me when she already had you."

"How could you think that? She's been devoted to you for years. We share only our concern for you."

"Concern?" Bronte heckled and a wiliness darkened his eyes. "It made complete sense to me once I thought about it. She's good. You're good. And both of you want to live by God's divine laws. Except that you couldn't keep your hands off her."

"I wish you could see yourself. Jealousy does nothing but make fools out of men. You love her so much you can't come to terms with her purity."

Brandishing his sword, Bronte winged Athos's weapon off the ground and caught it. "Take it. Defend yourself."

"I haven't dishonoured you. You're just angry that the plan you hatched with Anne backfired. You're displacing your anger on me."

Bronte thrust the pommel into Athos's ribcage, bumping him backward into a low stone wall.

"Stop this and listen to me!" Athos took the sword in self-defence. "Demi left her gloves by mistake. She visited me last week because she was concerned you were becoming distant. She had been sick and you didn't go to her. What else was she to think? Now, here you are, wanting to kill me for a tryst that never happened. I wouldn't deceive you after all our years of friendship."

"But the gloves ..."

"She left them because her hands were full of borrowed books."

Bronte growled like a cornered animal and almost pushed Athos over the stone. Athos grappled for balance and better words. "What did Demi say to you at Agape Lake? Tell me."

"She refused to talk to me." Bronte pointed his sword inches from Athos's heart.

"You can't give up. She loves you."

"Tame your tongue." Bronte aimed for the throat and finally caused Athos to lose his balance.

Laid out on the short wall, Athos deflected the sword with his forearm. "Ask her for her promise. Send her your proposal in a letter. A poem. I'll help you write it."

"So she is your muse?"

"Of course not."

"Then who?"

"Some things men don't share with anyone, even their closest friends."

Bronte again targeted the heart. "Don't lie to me."

"No more than you've lied to me." Athos grabbed the blade. "We're allowed a few secrets."

"Swear you haven't touched her."

"On my eternal salvation, I have not."

Bronte relaxed his aim, allowing Athos to let go of the blade and stand up.

"She'll say no to me," Bronte said.

"Not if you put your heart into it."

"Bronte!" A brusque voice yelled from a second-story window facing the courtyard. "Athos? Are you two bickering again?"

Bronte's father, Jean Claude, leaned out the window and bore the all-too-familiar expression of his son, a deep wrinkle between knitted brows. "Good Lord. There's no time for that! Hurry inside, both of you. Farther Turre is ill. You must go to him. Quickly."

# A New Confessor

Father Turre's room in the rectory smelled of incense and fever. Carrying an empty water basin, the priest's assistant met Athos and Bronte at the door. The servant shook his head, his eyes downcast, and scurried off into the dark hallway.

A single candle by the bedside cast a ghost-like pall over Turre. Athos touched the priest's cheek, searing with heat, and dabbed Turre's brow with a lukewarm rag by his pillow. Bronte lit a second candle and brought it to the bed. The priest's face, like clay, paled in the flickering light. Athos answered Bronte's question before it was spoken.

"I saw him less than two weeks ago completely well." Athos held a hand under Turre's nose. "We spoke in the library."

Turre's chest rattled with an uneasy exhale, and he began to wheeze.

"Father." Athos knelt at the bedside. "It's Bronte and me."

The corner of Turre's eyes wrinkled and his eyelids creased like thin paper. He blinked to attention, although his eyes were bloodshot from fever. Athos's knowledge of maladies was slim. He had known of epidemics that decimated villages and families and had feared the spread of sickness in his own realm. But Athos believed this sudden illness seemed different. He scanned Turre's skin for evidence that something besides nature or God's wrath was to blame. Athos shared an identical worried glance with Bronte.

"My young men." Turre garbled through a phlegm-filled throat. "The light hurts my eyes."

Bronte sat the candle on a pedestal sconce and stood back. Athos took the priest's hand and discovered his arms and torso were frigid. Turre's fever was only in his head.

"Father, you're as cold as a north wind." Athos sent Bronte out to find an extra cover.

"Am I?" Turre responded after a long delay, when it seemed he had sunk into delirium. "I feel quite warm."

"Your head, yes. What day did you become ill?"

"I can't remember. What day is it?" He tried to focus, blinking bleary-eyed at Athos's features. "You look so much like your father." Turre then focused on the ceiling and rambled a few words of Latin. "I must tell you something, you and Bronte. Your bond is at risk."

Bronte slipped back into the room behind Athos and handed over another blanket. Athos said to the side, "He's delirious."

The priest raised his voice. "I've had a vision. It concerns you!" He pointed to Bronte then Athos. "Both of you."

Athos tucked the priest's cold arm beneath the cover and spread the extra blanket. "Tell us later. Don't talk now. Build up your strength."

"You—Bronte—are as close to Athos as a brother." Turre's wheezing sped up. "Brothers have complicated relationships."

"Not completely delirious," Athos said. Bronte's blank reaction conveyed a thousand words. Athos stood, placing a hand on Bronte's shoulder. He shrugged it off.

The priest reared his head from the pillow by an inch. "In my vision, something comes between you."

Level-headed Turre rarely spoke of visions and superstition, as many common people did. Quite the opposite, Turre had instilled in Athos a healthy skepticism of religious men whose spirituality was defined by evil. The priest's declaration set Athos on edge.

"Go on," Bronte said.

Athos baulked. "Don't encourage this."

Turre gurgled from his chest. "You're not children any longer. In my dream, you think you're untouchable. But a force, I can't describe it any other way, splits you apart. It drives a wedge between you."

Athos shook his head. "Father—"

"He's speaking the truth," Bronte said, slightly louder than necessary.

"Don't let this evil break you apart." Turre's hands writhed under the blanket, and his eyes darted from Athos to Bronte. "Pledge your loyalty to each other. Do it here while I witness."

"Our bond is stronger than brothers," Athos said in earnest, kneeling close to the priest. Bronte remained quiet.

"It'll need to stay so, to survive."

"Survive?" Bronte said, dismissing Athos's admonishing stare. "Survive what?"

"A separation from God." The priest sunk into the bed as if all the breath and blood had spilled out of him. "Promise me. Seek out a confessor soon to cleanse your hearts. Especially you, Bronte. You're the most vulnerable."

Athos shook his head and patted Turre's face with the rag again. "But *you're* our confessor."

"I'm dying."

Athos clenched the rag and felt compelled to protest, except the priest closed his eyes and continued at half the volume. "Father de Breuil will hear your confessions. Go to him. It's of utmost importance."

Bronte raised a wary eyebrow. "You've seen him?"

But Turre seemed halfway to the other world.

Athos's voice was useless. Inwardly, he reeled at the priest's plainspoken death sentence. On top of it, Turre's suggestion to confess to Father de Breuil complicated everything. How could he? He'd tossed aside good sense with Anne too many times already. His gossiping and fighting with Bronte didn't help matters either. Turre would have given him a stern lecture; Father de Breuil might forbid contact with his sister.

Bronte moved backward toward the door. "We shouldn't stay. We have no idea what kind of illness he's got, and it could infect us both."

"If it's contagious," Athos said, still bothered by his instincts.

"I think you're delirious now," Bronte said, a hand on the door.

"Just go." Athos's patience ran out. "Do what you need to do."

"You mean, go confess?" Bronte's sarcasm hung in the feverish air.

Athos rubbed his face. "No, Bronte. Just go."

"What about you?"

"I'm taking him to Valliere in the morning. He'll be more comfortable there."

"And invite a plague into your home? Have at it." Bronte opened the door.

"Wait." Athos reached Bronte before he left. He suspected Turre's strange warning had emptied the room more than the illness. "Come see me tomorrow. I'll have something written for Demi by then."

As soon as Bronte was gone, the candle he lit fizzled out.

•   •   •

Only once before in Athos's memory had Valliere been so quiet—the death of his father. In the months leading up to that night, Athos ate little and slept less than his usual state of partial insomnia. None of the servants outlasted Athos's stamina. The death of his father was the first incomprehensible tragedy of Athos's manhood. His mother's death occurred when he was a little boy and was softened by doting friends and distance. As a lady in waiting, she'd spent most of her time at court. After his father's passing, Athos spent weeks alone in his room, reading scripture and writing verse that only saw light when he burned them.

Turre's oncoming death uprooted the old pain. The creep of death was like spilled ink, impossible to contain and black as a moonless night. Athos knew his priest was actively dying. His pale skin, his sallow eyes, every symptom signaled collapse. From what? Athos fretted with uncertainty. Instead of scripture, he collected every apothecary and remedy journal from his library and poured over them, a sentinel at the priest's side. Athos burned taper after taper to read the volumes of possible ailments and cures.

The symptoms were multiple and inconsistent with one illness. Hot head, cold body, yellow skin, tangled breathing, tremors. They indicated unnatural causes or the symptoms of withdrawal from an elixir. Possibly poison. From where? Turre never drank wine at meals or over-indulged at village festivals, where even the most pious abandoned their morals for a while.

Athos concluded Turre's condition and the visions seemed connected—due to an invisible hand, an intangible spectre.

Athos sent for Bronte after three days.

"We must summon Father de Breuil for last rites." They stood in the doorway to Turre's dying place. Bronte looked thin, too.

"That's all fine and good, if anyone could find him." Bronte covered his own mouth after Turre coughed weakly.

Athos pulled Bronte into the hall, one of the few times he'd left Turre's room since placing the priest there. "You must find him. Where's Anne? With him?"

"No one seems to know. Rumour is they went to the abbey at Saint Germain in Paris for a short pilgrimage, but I can't confirm it."

"Now? When everyone knows Father Turre is deathly ill?" From the hall, Athos walked out onto a balcony laid with stone. He took deep breaths of the fresh evening air. "This is the most important thing I'll ask of you for some time. Find Father de Breuil. Bring him here. And bring Anne with him."

"I'd call that a little selfish."

Athos clenched his fist, although his first reaction was a slap. "You wouldn't have come today if I hadn't sent for you. Don't you have any compassion?"

"Hold on, I've been poking around for de Breuil and Anne for days."

"And no one has seen either one?"

"Not so much as a lock of hair."

Athos went into Turre's room for his journal and met Bronte back in the hall. "I have something for you." Athos removed a folded note inside the pages and placed it within Bronte's reach. "Your poem. For Demi."

Bronte snatched it and paced as he read. A slant in his eyes told Athos he was pleased, yet Bronte's face morphed into ice at the last line. "This is her. Exactly."

"I know." Athos wasn't bragging. After he had written it, deep in the nights of Turre's death watch, he could scarcely believe the words had come from inside him. The verse was simple and beautiful, like Demi.

"*You,* my sovereign. How can you be so—so perfect."

Athos refused to take the bait. Exhausted, he rubbed a creeping ache in his shoulders. "And how did you become like this?"

"Like what?" Bronte crumpled the note into a trouser pocket.

"So jealous of me."

Using the heel of his hand, Bronte knocked the ache back into Athos's shoulder. "I'm not."

"Then why are you this way?" Athos threw up his hands and reached for Bronte's pocket. "If you don't want my help, then don't take it."

Bronte batted his hand away. "It'll work. As for the last rites, I'll search high and low for de Breuil. On my word."

Bronte failed to return before Turre's death two nights later. At the dying hour, Athos raced to the cathedral in Blois by himself to find a nun to administer the sacrament. It was better than nothing. After the nun left, Athos, himself in a death-like state, sat with the body for several hours. He felt cold inside and out. For the loss of his confessor, for his friend's short-comings, and for the vision he knew clouded the future.

Part

# II

# FROM MAN, WOMAN

*O cunning Love! with tears thou keep'st me blind,*
*Lest eyes well-seeing thy foul faults should find.*
*~ William Shakespeare*

# The Sun

"I thought I'd find you here." Anne showed up out of nowhere inside the Blois Cathedral, blocking the light from Athos's favourite stained glass window, the Garden of Eden.

Her sudden appearance at the end of the pew should have startled him. Here, where he'd spent a lifetime worshipping, Athos was praying near the candle lit for Turre. In the week since the priest's death, the nave echoed hollowly for lack of its spiritual leader. With her, it rang in rejoice. Her presence ignited Athos's hope.

He grabbed her hand and drew her into his body on the pew. His kiss landed on warm and receptive lips.

"You missed me." Her words were as perfect as his relief.

For the first time since he'd sent Bronte to find her, he let himself relax. He gently held her head in his hands and took stock of the beautiful reason. "Where have you been? Do you know—"

"Of Turre's death? We left when he was well. It's shocking."

"Untimely." He kissed her again, wishing he could forget his grief long enough to give her a proper, and more sensual, welcome. Yet the eyes of every statue in the church seemed fixed on them.

The warmth of her next to him helped. He was self-conscious that he hadn't lit a candle for Anne's safe return, next to the one in remembrance of Turre. As an afterthought, he realized he'd also forgotten Bronte.

"I've been searching for you. You and your brother," Athos said, enjoying the light in her eyes.

Anne's smile was subtle, downplayed to match her grey travelling clothes. "How could you be looking for us and praying at the same time?"

"Bronte has been searching for you, or at least, I think he is. I asked him to." Athos rubbed her gloved hands. "Tell me where you were, or is that a secret, too, like you?"

"You're still after my story?" Fatigue washed over her, making her head list for a moment. Then she inhaled and her grace revived. From her coat pocket, she produced a palm-sized book. "For you."

The thin volume looked new. Athos turned it over in his hands, rubbing the leather, absorbing the gift. "You were thinking of me on your journey." Secretly, he wished he had something for her. He smiled instead. "Thank you."

"You don't even know what it is yet. Open it. Read me a line." Her sharp blue eyes insisted he follow instructions.

The second he began to skim the passages, the words pulled him in. Although in English, the verse revived his passion—for poetry. He spoke a few lines out of the simple desire to hear them out loud. "*It is my love that keeps mine eye awake, Mine own true love that doth my rest defeat, to play the watchman ever for thy sake.*"

"And do you?" Her fingers swirled across his thigh.

He laid a hand on hers to keep it from meandering up his leg too far. "Do I lie awake all night thinking of you? If you'd stop running off, I might." He wanted to overtake her, make the ground shake beneath them. "This poet, Shakespeare, I want *you* to read me every line. Your English is better. So, when you're in my company, the book will be yours."

He wrapped her hands around the book rather than his leg.

The corners of her mouth flinched. Her disappointment was justified. His restraint confounded him, too. But this wasn't the place for blurring lines, despite her habit of finding pleasure everywhere.

"Father Turre counselled me my entire life." He held on to her hands in a prayerful embrace, the book between her palms. "Ever since I can remember, he gave me advice. It was of greater importance after my father died. My father trusted him more than anyone."

She ran the bottom of her chin across his shoulder and stopped underneath his ear. "I know what it's like to lose a trusted friend."

He turned his head closer to hear her breathing. The fragrance of her hair, lingering notes of honeysuckle, took him back to his less-than-pure thoughts. "Why have you come here?"

"To see you, of course."

"In my grief." And longing, he admitted.

"I couldn't stay away."

A draft drew them closer, and he placed the book of sonnets on the bench. "The last time we were together, you said that you'd tell me your story. I want to hear it."

She shifted in her seat and stared behind him toward a grotto of the Virgin Mary. "This isn't the place."

He glanced to the Virgin, a statue that was installed when he was coming of age. The piece was always a dilemma to him, a sacred image he revered but was also enthralled by, because of Mary's beauty.

"She's amazing, isn't she?" He squeezed her hands again and refocused Anne's attention on him. "What could be more perfect than a place of God to share yourself?"

Anne fidgeted with her gloves but not for long. Her mischievousness returned. "And what about you? When we spoke last, you promised to share a secret with me. Your muse."

Athos wanted to laugh, a little because of her devilish look, a little because he had forgotten his promise, and a little because of his embarrassment to admit the truth.

"You," he chuckled, "don't miss any details."

"Why should I? I'm as intrigued by you as you are by me."

"Then you should have already guessed what my muse is, if you're as half as smart as I think."

She squinted and bit her lower lip. "Well ..."

"Come, come. Don't disappoint me." He snuggled, wrapping an arm around her shoulders. Dangerous, he knew, for even the conversation was making him want her. If her intellect was any indication, her sexual prowess promised to be legendary.

"Your muse isn't a woman."

"You sound very certain." He inhaled her honeysuckle scent.

Her body tensed and her eyes narrowed. She seemed determined to figure him out, bit by bit.

"You also aren't taken with objects—art, relics, land. Other than books, you don't seem to covet treasure or wealth."

Her chest quickened its rise and fall, and her excitement over the puzzle made him hungry for her. He hoped her cunning would reveal his secret. He kissed her earlobe. "Keep thinking."

"But you're very principled. To a point. You're not a flawless man, but a man with a centre. And that centre is strong." She lifted her eyes from his face, and clarity swept over her expression. Lit by the stained glass of the depiction of Eden, she glowed in triumph.

"Say it, my seraphim," Athos said. "What is my muse?"

"God is, Fere. God is your inspiration."

He met her lips with a force greater than himself. Her discovery derailed his composure. *How can she understand me so well?* His body wanted to know, and his weight plunged them flat on the pew, spreading her onto the cushion. He thoughtlessly let his hands explore her, seeking the forbidden heat simmering under her clothes.

She untucked his shirt-tail and slipped her gloved hands inside to graze his back. She passed into his trousers and to the front, where she cooed in approval. She whispered *yes*, and he longed to oblige. Every impulse seemed possible.

Every dream between them of total surrender, he wanted to create.

*Right here ... now ... in my sanctuary. God's sanctuary.*

He broke reluctantly from her mouth, pulled up her stroking hands, and took a deep breath. The desire on her face was sweet lust. He wanted to taste the apple and feed on the banquet. But God said no. His house thundered in disapproval.

He sat them upright. She tried pulling him back down. His eyes relayed his thoughts: *I want you, but* ... At least they had stayed fully clothed, he rationalised.

"Anne," he said as gently as he could, a tender let-down, as if the moon were telling the sun good-night. "Another time—"

"You can't deny what we feel." Pleading, she used her slight weight to bring him close again. "Love is creation. We're closer to God."

"I feel it, yes. You're a beautiful temptation. But I'm a flawed man. Had I met you a year ago, there's no question how this would end." He untangled a strand of blond from her moist lips. "But I'm different now, and I want you in a different way. Do you understand?"

She nodded, first down, then to the statue of the Virgin Mary. "Your faith is blind belief of the mind. I believe love is blind devotion of the heart."

Her mind dazzled him. Everything he could have wanted in a woman he found in Anne. Beauty, intelligence, sensuality. It seemed counter-instinctual to wait. But in his heart, the reason for his restraint held strong, for the moment.

"The direction of my life is important. I must honour both faith and love." He kissed her again and lingered at her lips. "I will please you, Anne, in many, many ways. I promise. Let me show you at the right time."

"Maybe our time has passed." She stood abruptly, smoothed her skirt, and backed to the end of the pew.

"Not if we've never gotten started," he said and aimed to grab her hand, but the seraphim slipped through his grasp.

She never broke eye contact. "Use your muse. See if He," she pointed upward, "can win me over."

# The Poet

The challenge lay before him. Anne expected a poetic seduction.

For several days, he read and reread the book of Shakespeare. He was struck by the sonnets' melancholy imagery, more moving than most of the poems Athos kept in his library. Even in translation, the words depicted a man in longing and pain. Shakespeare had captured the essence of love and heartache. Themes of obsession and betrayal threaded the work together.

Inspired, Athos tried to write. *What does Anne want to hear? What is my heart saying?* In truth, he knew too little to understand her. He felt their attraction, primarily physical, was a seedling. It required ripening. He needed to coax her out with sun, warmth, and starlight. Lyrical promises. His heart must decorate the page.

He plotted to deliver his secret notes of seduction on Sundays. Father de Breuil wouldn't suspect. Because of Turre's passing, Athos had no spiritual home. His presence now at Father de Breiul's services in Averdon wouldn't make anyone think twice. He pre-arranged to pass poems to Genue or Margot before Mass and wait for Anne's reaction, sitting behind her in the pew farthest from the front balustrade. Each short verse ended the same: *Look back for me. I shall meet you wherever you ask.*

In full formal dress during the onset of summer, he endured four of Father de Breuil's sermons. With each twist of Anne's hair, Athos prayed she would turn around. Moments before communion, on the fourth Sunday, she finally dipped her chin into her collar, looked behind her, and locked intently on his eyes.

His body quavered. She was the diamond, and he was the cut.

She fanned an envelope under her nose.

As soon as Mass concluded, he waited for the envelope's delivery by the stoup. He took more pleasure than usual greeting anyone who approached. After a half hour, the church emptied, and soon his patience vanished, too. He started to think he had imagined her blue-eyed response. Perhaps the last month without friends—visitors, Bronte, a mentor—had warped his perception.

He had asked around Blois for Bronte several times, and once had talked to his brother Racine, but the most news anyone had was that Bronte had left unexpectedly. Each day of Bronte's absence, Athos grew more sullen. He regretted sending Bronte off before they had smoothed over their bumps. Their disagreement over Demi was probably keeping Bronte from rushing back.

"Have you heard?" Father de Breuil slipped an arm under Athos's elbow and shuffled them toward the church study. Catching himself from tripping, Athos scanned the church foyer again to make sure he hadn't missed Anne.

Athos carefully hid his frown from the priest. "Have I heard what?"

"That Cardinal Richelieu is sending a replacement for Father Turre."

Athos stopped short of the study door. The news was significant enough for him to forget why he was at this church in the first place. Almost. "How did you hear?"

"My superiors in Paris sent a message a few days ago." Father de Breuil continued to guide Athos toward the door. "I'm sure they'll be contacting you any day."

"Is it someone you know?" Through the threshold, Athos got his first glimpse of the interior of the priest's dim study. Because of their strict code of poverty, Athos assumed most priests had few possessions, but de Breuil's office was cluttered with books and papers and faded, unframed paintings on canvas. It was disorderly or, more specifically, neglected. Dusty light from a high rectangular window filled the room and a loamy odour hung over a hodge-podge desk.

"Ah, yes, here it is." Father de Breuil found the letter under a frayed book. "It says the priest is Father Luc. He'll bring with him an assistant and a collection of antique swords, which he may need to place in your care."

"Swords?" Now Athos was thoroughly distracted. Weren't worldly possessions surrendered?

"The letter says he was once a Musketeer."

Athos backed into a cushionless chair and dropped into it. Another puff of dust filled the daylight streaming in. "Can Musketeers be priests?"

"Any man, well, let me say, any man *with a calling*, can be a priest. It's a matter of time and study. An advocate doesn't hurt either."

Athos had never given it much thought, whether priests might be men experienced in swordplay or military duty. Maybe war equipped a man with more compassion. Looking up, Athos wondered what de Breuil's path had been. He was middle-aged, and his eyes were droopy. A smattering of grey framed his temples. The clergyman's smile gave off the impression that he could read a person's mind.

"We shall miss your faithful attendance here," de Breuil said, patting Athos on the hand.

"Father?" Athos took the cordiality as an opportunity. "May I discuss an important issue with you?"

"Of course, stay." The priest pulled up a plain chair for himself.

"I would like to spend time with your sister."

Father de Breuil folded his hands and rested them on his knees. His eyes narrowed. "She's not spoken for, if that's the information you seek."

"That's not exactly it."

"If you're in need of a wife, I have the authority as her guardian."

Athos struggled to pick the right words. "She seems to be evading my requests for her company."

"If you and your family so desire, a marriage can be arranged.

Unfortunately," he shuffled his feet, "Anne's much too *wily* for my liking."

"To state it mildly." Athos immediately wished his comment would float off in the dust.

Father de Breuil bolted to his feet, and his chair tottered. "Monsieur Athos, as her protector, I'm entitled to my opinion of Anne's behaviour. As a potential suitor, it may be wiser to keep your opinions to yourself."

"I misspoke," he said, shaking his head. "But I'm assuming she has no dowry, and my affections could lead to marriage."

The priest repositioned himself on the chair. "Not to seem blunt, but a sovereign's right outweighs any so-called affection."

"But when I marry, affection will be important." Athos stood and placed a hand on the priest's shoulder. "I need your help. Simply encourage her to spend time with me. It's not outside of my authority to ask. There's no point going further if she won't agree to see me beforehand."

"Today, you're blessed." Father de Breuil sighed and produced another letter from the mess burying his desk. "She asked me to give you this."

Athos snatched the note and started to break the seal, but the priest reclaimed hold of a corner.

"Monsieur ... Comte de la Fere. If you'd indulge me, please hear my advice. You may not be interested in exercising your right to marry anyone you want, but in this case, you should reconsider. As you seem to have discovered, Anne's sometimes difficult. If you wait around to make it—*her*—perfect, you may never end up where you want to go."

Athos bowed and left after a quiet *adieu*. He regretted the awkward nature of the conversation, but his mission was accomplished. As he stepped outside into a burning afternoon sun to read Anne's note, it dawned on him that he might never tire of her boldness.

# Bitter and Sweet

Anne's note read: *Your poems whet my appetite for your company. Meet me tomorrow at the monastery at Marmoutier in Alsace an hour after dawn. In anticipation, Anne* Athos felt more happiness than he had the year his father granted him possession of a family sword two generations old. Anne's request out-shined any steel heirloom.

Risking rumours of his uncharacteristic joy, he rode to Blois, strutted through the open-air market, and bestowed glad tidings on many of the local merchants, who looked on in surprise at his open purse. Athos bought a bouquet of wildflowers, a silk handkerchief, and a bag of apples. The maidens and young girls fawned and giggled, showering him with salutations of purple words that covered the bachelor prince in royal cloth. He basked in their grand favour.

The air smelled rich with the bounties of the season, early peas and daisies, and the signs of oncoming summer appeared everywhere, especially in the women's lack of neckerchiefs and long sleeves. He smiled more than he had in weeks, until he saw a young woman, covered head to toe in grey, who snaked around a corner with a bread basket.

When he caught up with Demi, her shoulders and head drooped, and a near-permanent frown creased her face.

"You miss Bronte," Athos confirmed and guided her into a private walled garden. He demanded she eat an apple before he started in with questions, and he dabbed the silk scarf on her chin to wipe the juice. Even in her pain, she was beautiful. "I suppose this means you haven't heard from him either," he said.

She nodded and took a few small bites.

"It's my fault." Athos ground a fist into his thigh. "He left unhappy because of me. Left because I pushed him away. We should have cleared the air first, but we didn't."

"I saw him. He came to me before Turre died, on his way to find Father de Breuil."

"And no word from him since?"

"None."

"I'm so sorry, Demi."

"Minor, compared to the rest."

"The rest?"

"I should have guessed he didn't tell you." She stared at a bite mark in the apple. "It's his father. Bronte never told his father about me."

Her words sounded like a foreigner's. *How could Bronte keep Demi, his true love, a secret?*

"That's illogical," Athos said. "He wants to marry you."

Sadness washed behind Demi's eyes. "Did he recently mention his brother to you?"

"Not recently, though he did say many weeks ago that Racine had asked you to marry him, and Bronte told me he'd beaten him off, though I believed he was half-joking."

"His father has arranged for Racine to marry me—" Demi broke off and crumpled into Athos's lap, sobbing.

"I've never heard such absurdities." Athos stroked her hair. "Demi, no one in all the province is blind to Bronte's affection for you. It's impossible."

"He hid it ... from his family," she said between gulps of air. "He knew his father would object because of my family. I lack the stature to marry a magistrate's first-born son. Now, it's no use."

"How did this all come about? Bronte was intent on settling the arrangements before he left." *Though too hesitantly.*

"He tried, but it was too late. He and his father argued about me for several days. After that, Bronte disappeared."

Athos clung to the bench, ashamed by his own self-centredness. He had missed every clue. No wonder Bronte had been scarce the final days of Turre's life. His friend was trying to salvage his romance. Athos hadn't bothered to see Bronte's life.

"Did you forgive him for the episode at the lake?" Athos thought the answer was obvious.

"Because of this, I did." Demi removed her wrist-satchel and dug out a wisp of paper. Obviously unfolded countless times, it seemed held together by faith and a few fibres. She read the poem aloud. Hearing his own words, Athos swallowed back tears.

He placed a hand on hers after she carefully replaced the

note to its safe place. "He loves you so very much. I'm glad you gave him a second chance."

"It doesn't matter now. We'll both stew in regret and be miserable in marriages we don't want."

"I doubt Bronte will abide by his father's wishes. He's apt to duel his way out of it, even if it's his brother."

"They've already arranged another match for Bronte. The winds shifted very quickly for us." A cool breeze fluttered Demi's hair ribbon.

"And he settled? What am I saying! Did *the woman* settle? What mademoiselle would have him, save a saint?" Athos hooked a cord of her satchel with his index finger and tugged. Demi didn't acknowledge his sideways compliment.

"A very rich one. My cousin, Margot."

Athos didn't know whether to laugh or cry. On one hand, Athos suffered because of a lack of family. On another, his dearest friends suffered at the hands of theirs.

"I've seen Margot every Sunday this month," Athos said in monotone. "She didn't mention any of this."

"Then they'll make a nice pair." But Demi's joke ended with her face planted in her hands. Athos embraced her and murmured a few well-meaning words.

"Thank you," Demi said, putting distance between them and flattening her crushed satchel.

"I'd intervene if I thought it'd do any good, but my sovereignty has its limits." He gathered her hands.

"You've done your part." She raised the satchel to her lips and kissed it. She rose from the bench, and at the opening in the garden wall, left a parting thought. "Bronte was right to trust your voice."

She vanished before he could take credit, not that he had intended to. She knew the poem had been his.

Awestruck by Demi's intelligence and grace, Athos lost track of time by himself in the garden. The afternoon became quieter than a church on a snowy winter's evening. But the birds sang, and his thoughts circled back around to Anne. He ate an apple and watched a small garter snake twist underneath a flowering hedge of honeysuckle.

# 11

# The Honey House

The night proved restless. Two emotions tortured him in the dark—excitement about his rendezvous with Anne and unease because of his argument with Bronte and the passing of his priest. By the time he arrived at the monastery at Marmoutier, he yearned for control. He wanted to win Anne's game of love and prove to himself that his destiny was still somewhat within his power, not just God's.

The church was empty, so he lit a candle and said a prayer. *God give me strength.* It couldn't hurt to ask God to support his battle for love.

Outlying sections of the monastery grounds were open to visitors. He wandered outside and spotted a few monks gardening and tending the dovecote. He didn't bother asking them if they'd seen Anne. He knew if she wanted to be found, she would be.

Having left the Shakespeare book at home, he simply brought himself, in a plain white shirt and dark riding pants, and a bouquet of pink tulips from the market.

He rounded a thick hedge at a far corner of the property and discovered her back to him. Her hair spilled loosely down her back, no ribbons or lace. She faced a small wooden shed about the size of a horse stall, nothing more than four walls on short stilts. It had a ramp instead of steps and horizontal slats instead of windows. A soft hum sweetened the air.

"Do you hear them?" When she turned, he noticed a twig of honeysuckle in her hand. She wore an informal dress in soft blue adorned by large brocade buttons up the middle. She wasn't wearing gloves.

"Thank you for responding to my poems." He had spent much of his sleepless night deciding what he would say to her. He decided to heed her brother's advice and be more forthcoming with her. "I want to see more of you, Anne. I'd write a thousand poems if it meant you'd see me again."

"Ah, your poems." She closed her eyes and inched toward him. He opted to play the pursued and circled to the door of the shed.

"The way I see it," he said, regaining her attention as the grass rustled under his feet, "is that you've gotten what you wanted. You've seen my château, you've looked through my books, you've eaten my food, and, to top it off, you've played with my muse. Now, it's my turn."

He held out the bouquet and waited until she crossed over and took it. She added the vine of honeysuckle to the pink tulips.

"For a kiss," she said, inhaling the blooms, "I'll grant you your wish."

He slowly encircled her waist with both hands, enjoying her permission, and discovered that she was not wearing a corset. It was as if she had come to him in her nightdress. Her waist was soft underneath his caresses.

He leaned toward her lips but diverted at the last second to nip her earlobe instead. "You owe me your story first," he said.

She jerked back and broke away. He liked the intensity in her eyes. It aroused his hunter's instinct.

"I owe you nothing." She flung the bouquet to the grass, scattering petals, and tried to dodge out of his reach. He reclaimed her tightly by the waist.

"You want me, but you don't want me to know you." In his grasp, Athos felt her struggle was half-hearted. "Anne, let me know you."

He let her go and threw his hands up in surrender. Her flight lasted but a few feet. Backing off, he accidentally bumped into the shed's ramp and lost his balance for a moment. He wasn't above chasing her, but he needed to show he'd wait her out, stubborn or not.

"Something tells me I may have a shred more patience than you do," he said, one foot on the ramp.

She huffed in disapproval and grabbed the bouquet from the ground. "Have you been stung by a bee before?"

"Once or twice." He was gratified that she hadn't run away.

"Nonetheless," she said and motioned toward the shed, "we shouldn't tempt them."

At the top of the ramp, Athos ducked through the low

opening of the door. A few steps inside and he stood in the centre of the long, rectangular honey house. Stripes of light shined through the wide slats on one side and warmed his back. Beneath each slat was a shelf lined with open jars of honey, and the thick, sweet aroma tickled his nostrils. The sunlight glistened with amber.

A smile overtook him. "This is why—"

"I smell like honey?" she interrupted from a few steps away. She smiled back.

"Honeysuckle," he said.

"There's a field of it below the monastery. The bees gather nectar there." She laid the bouquet on a shelf and leaned toward a jar. "If you breathe deeply, you can smell the fragrance of the flower."

He obliged, but he also regretted being cornered. She blocked the only way out, and the heat, the flowery aroma, and her proximity side-tracked his good intentions. She could easily persuade him to forgo her life story while their desires took over.

"Now that we're in private," he managed to say, "I'm all ears." *And mouth and tongue and racing heart.*

She sighed and looked down at her feet on the soft pinewood floor. Until then, he hadn't noticed she was barefoot.

"What do you want to know?" she asked.

Finally, when he had her where he wanted her, he couldn't think of what to ask. Maybe if he thought of pruning roses? Instead, the rose he had in mind confounded his ability to speak. "Your life ... I want to hear about it."

She moved in face to face and spoke in a hush. He detected a tremble in her voice, unlike he'd heard before. "If I tell you, Fere, will you swear to secrecy?"

Her lips quivered. He struggled to nod without melting into them.

Her breathing became shallow. "I was born in England. My mother was French and so was my father, but he passed himself off as English to earn money. The trades for furriers were more lucrative there than in France. He died in the stockade after he wouldn't agree to serve in the English army. You wouldn't blame him. No Frenchman worth his birthright would stoop so low." She wound a curl around her fingertip, which turned red at once. "When he died, my mother was an outcast. Her English was very poor, although my brother and I could speak fluently. She found work for Gregori and me as servants, chattel more like it. I still have scars from the whippings. An enclave of Jesuits took pity on Gregori because he expressed a calling to God. My mother went mad from our situations, but her final act was to beg the Jesuits to take me in with my brother. They reluctantly agreed and allowed us to live in the shadow of their lives."

Athos grasped her despair. "Being among them couldn't have been ideal. Your beauty ..."

Her lips pursed in anger, and she finally unwound the hair from her finger. "Yes, my beauty." She pressed her back against a shelf of honey, and the jars tipped slightly forward. "I couldn't hide. One man in particular wouldn't ignore me."

"A *priest?*" Athos's yearning transformed into anger.

"You sound shocked that a man of the faith is corruptible. Every man is corruptible." Anne nudged the shelf, which tilted more. A few of the jars began to slide forward, and Athos stretched out his arms to keep the jars in place, bringing him inches from her. He sensed her pain and her magnetic draw. "What about your brother? Was there nothing he could do?"

Anne laughed from her throat. "I took care of *him*, Fere. I took care of *him*."

"How long did you endure the priest's advances?" He swallowed back the thoughts of her under a man in robes, writhing in disgust, exposed to the forbidden knowledge she so skilfully brandished now to her advantage.

"Years. Then Gregori took his orders, and I followed."

"Does he know?"

She glanced to a jar. A thin layer of wax covered the top. "Good and evil co-exist. Aquinas wrote volumes on the subject. The Jesuits had a vast library."

"You sought refuge in books, poems." Athos saw darkness and light in her eyes, memories filled with pain. "I wish for you a different story."

"Why? If this one brings me to you?" She came off the shelf and it righted itself, making him relax and drop his arms. She pressed a thumbprint on a jar. "Ancient people believe that honey is an aphrodisiac."

"And do you?"

"Without a doubt. It's why I come here." Her eyes were playing him. She'd changed the subject, but he was tangled in her history. A woman soiled under God's watch. *What kind of God would do this to her?*

"Fere, don't be sad. I live for the sweetness of life, not in regret."

She selected a jar from a shelf and stirred it with her finger. "The monks are superstitious and believe the sunlight will burn off the honey's impurities."

Her finger dripped with golden syrup, and she dragged the excess across the rim like a knife. "Would you like a taste?"

Everything else but her fell away in the next few minutes of his life. Every pulse point in his body throbbed. She painted his lips with a thin gloss of honey, and the sweetness and salt of her finger coated his tongue. Then she did the same on her own lips. Setting the jar aside, she unbuttoned her bodice and opened the front to him. The buds of her breasts were hard, and she smiled when a faint moan escaped him. He desperately searched for his voice.

"Please, not here." His plea fell from his lips, hollow of truth. He wanted to taste her, to gorge, and be devoured in return.

They fused together in the next breath, and the kiss on her lips delivered the sweet aphrodisiac. She dipped her fingers in another jar and painted her breasts and guided his mouth to them. His tongue flicked the tip of each crest and she coated them again. His senses rocked with each delicious lick. His mouth and tongue. Her fingers and breasts. Every muscle tensed to take her, every sinew tuned to seek her pleasure spots, and the flavour of her skin overpowered his will.

He took control of the undressing. He bared her shoulders and landed kisses while she snuggled into his chest as her sleeves fell. His hand stopped at the black ribbon wrapped around one arm, the band on her that he remembered seeing at the lake. He kissed the ribbon, too, thinking it might be an injury from her sordid past.

"Don't," she said and her dress caught at her waist. Her eyes became sharp, yet he knew she wouldn't hold back. She lifted off his shirt to bare his chest against hers. The contact increased the heat in his centre to boiling. They were near the point of no return, and he wasn't giving God any say.

"Lie down for me," he said, croaking it out of his thick throat. Half-dressed, she lowered onto her back, her ribcage rising and falling faster than his heart could keep pace. Her hair on the wood floor splayed around her head and shoulders like an exotic fan. The image of her beneath him, near naked, vulnerable and ready, stabbed him with imminent need. He squeezed his eyes shut to slow his rampant arousal.

"It's been a long time," she said, with an air of sympathetic understanding, and he nodded and slowly opened his eyes. She gazed at the bulge between his legs and began to wriggle her dress down her hips.

"Wait." He couldn't control his body if she revealed the sweetest spot between her legs. "Let me first."

Before he could untie his waistband, she shook her head and pointed to a jar. He handed her the honey. Dangling the glass above her throat, she gingerly poured a fine line from her Adam's apple to navel, where she let it pool on the waves of her rapid breath.

"You have no idea what you do to me," he whispered. But he knew she did. She wanted to test his manhood, make him ache until his body snapped. He dropped to all fours and lapped up the sweet line. He made long, lazy passes with his tongue up and down her torso. His mouth took her from jawline to the swell of her belly. She worked his pants to his knees, and she whimpered a little when he lifted up.

The sunlight amplified the glow in her eyes. "You shouldn't keep such treasure hidden away in your château."

His confidence always spiked at his lovers' first encounters with him. He took her hand and started to bring it between his legs, but she held firm. "First, the honey," she purred.

She handed him the jar. He didn't need any other cues. He poured between his legs, and her mouth bestowed the blessing.

"Dear God." He uttered again and again, with each arch of his back, thinking He would strike the sinner where he knelt. Athos raised his arms, crucified by pleasure and guilt. Athos's morals said *stop*; his body said *plunder*. Her mouth anointed pleasure that he needed and wanted. And he wanted every drop. The warmth of her mouth and the smell of honeysuckle transformed his hunger into voraciousness. He believed his growing desire to take her equalled the need for sustenance after famine. The peak was so close, he grabbed her black ribbon and spoke out of desperation. "Let me inside."

She shimmied up to meet him, eye to eye, both of them kneeling in the golden power of the honey house. He kissed the liquid sugar from her lips and anticipated the final destination, the tender pocket no jar of honey could surpass. The dress, bunched around her middle, gave way with a few quick tugs.

In their embrace, he raced his thumb down her back and paused at the fine dust of hair at the base of her spine.

"*You have made me forget all my sorrows,*" he recited.

"The poet in you never dies." She naturally shivered as he smoothed both hands over the rise of her bottom and took a final pass of his mouth across her collarbone.

In his next deep kiss, he began to lay her back again, but strangely she resisted. Instead, she became rigid and silent, crushing into his front and protecting her flanks with her forearms. Her voice wavered. "Fere. Fere."

He quickly discovered why. She looked aghast at the slats, or rather, *through them.* The sunlight was blocked in several spots around the house. The breeze and light between the slats had been replaced by several sets of wide eyes.

One of the monks cleared his throat self-consciously the second the group was discovered.

Athos hugged Anne tighter and quickly drew up her dress to cover her back. Then he slammed a forearm several times between the shelves and bellowed, "*Be gone with you! Away!*" Several jars of honey hit the floor and shattered before the shadows turned to light.

His escape from God had been thwarted again.

# 12

# A New Priest

Once the monks had scurried away, Anne dashed half-dressed from the honey house. She left Athos sticky, hot, and uncomfortable from the waist down. Dejectedly, Athos rode alone to Agape Lake for a soak. It was just as well. The sign from God was clear. *I must wait.*

The day's heat and the ride made him sweat off most of the honey by the time he got to the lake, where the cool water and solitude relieved him. He bathed and relaxed in the knowledge that almost everyone else would be busy in the fields. He cursed his bad luck when a stranger emerged from the bushes, catching Athos thigh-high in the water, nude. A tall man in his greying years boomed with laughter from the bank.

"I've found it!" The man's eyes turned up at the corners. He immediately stripped to the waist and his middle shook as he chuckled. "You peasants know all the best watering holes."

Plunging in, Athos shrugged off the company. He surfaced to find the man sweating from the heat but expecting a conversation, so Athos begrudgingly took on his assigned role. "We peasants also know who makes the best wine in the village."

"Grand! Then you and I shall be friends." The fellow threw off his pants, waded up to his navel and submerged. After scrubbing his face and ears, he shook his short-cropped wiry grey hair like a happy dog. But the show was less fascinating to Athos than several significant scars on the visitor's chest, arms, and abdomen.

"Would wine help your old wounds?" Athos asked, baiting the man to tell his war stories.

"Oh, no," the visitor said, running a hand across his chest and arms. He flexed a bicep. "My body has God's resilience. And I've long given up serious swordplay. I would rather have decent wine for communion."

*Communion!*

Jolted out of his bad mood, Athos waded toward the man and startled him with a handshake.

"Father Luc?"

The priest looked Athos from side to side. "You've heard of me already?"

"I am Comte de la Fere, the sovereign of Berry. I've been told of your new appointment, and I sincerely apologise if I've given you the wrong impression of who I am."

Father Luc belly-laughed again, causing his double chin and ample stomach to shake in unison. "It's a fine sovereign who can partake of a good joke and the simpler pleasures of life, my son. We shall get along swimmingly." The pun made the priest laugh again as he returned a vigorous handshake.

"The cathedral has been desolate since Father Turre's passing," Athos said, aware his glances at the priest's scars might border on rude. "His death was a shock."

"How long had he been your confessor?"

"From adolescence on," Athos said, "and my father's and mother's as well."

"Grief fills your eyes," Father Luc said, folding his hands loosely across his bare middle. "To lose your father and your priest within such a short time is a great loss."

Athos had anticipated the priest's knowledge of his history. Still, the open book of his life felt tattered and private, and Athos turned out to the pond, hoping to hide some of the pain. Quiet ripples lapped around the void.

"My sympathies." Father Luc laid a warm hand on his shoulder. "Another time. We have many hours ahead to learn about each other."

Athos glanced back, nodded, and laid on his back to float. The honey was gone and so was the glow from his encounter with Anne. Father Luc splashed about or, more accurately, frolicked like a water-loving hound.

"When did you arrive?" Athos asked, swimming to shallower water to sit half-submerged. "I expected another message from Paris first."

"I often operate on my own schedule." The priest's guttural chuckles caught in the breeze between splashes. "As soon as I get orders, I go. It's hard to shake the soldier out of me."

Athos finally remembered. *The scars.* "Of course! A Musketeer! Your background is astonishing. I'd love to learn how a man goes from allegiance to country one day, to God the next."

The splashing ceased. Jutting his jaw sideways, Father Luc appeared to be staring through Athos rather than at him. "As if there's a difference."

"Now *you're* playing with *me*," Athos said, searching the priest for a sign of his former good humour.

"No." Father Luc's grey sideburns glistened with water droplets. Still, no smile. He started for the bank. "Like the Bible, a sword is a tool of devotion to both God and country."

"Easier to believe coming from a priest." Athos rose to dress and pulled on his pants from a heap on the uneven bank. "But you've got to admit that God may have had a little less to do with those scars."

"If He'd meant me to lead a quiet life of devotion, I would have," Father Luc said, ankle deep in water. He folded his hands over his middle, which was also feathered with grey hair. "They're marks of dedication to beliefs greater than myself."

"Come," Athos said, offering the priest a hand up from the incline. The priest was a good sign, Athos decided, and the timing of the clergyman's arrival was helping his outlook. "I want you to see my home. Valliere. And, call me Athos."

As soon as the two got dressed, they rode to the château, where Athos's servants were prepared for Father Luc's arrival. The priest's escorts, several lackeys from Paris, had arrived ahead of time with Father Luc's collection of swords.

The dozen weapons were laid out in the banquet room on the table rarely used for banquets. Athos marvelled at the set.

Swords of steel with bronze inlaid patterns and intricate re-lief. Many of the blades showed signs of battle, chinks and scratches; few were unmarked. Athos held up one missing a tip.

"What happened to this one?" Athos touched the blunt end and saw his deep-set curiosity in the reflection of the blade.

"Poor judgment." Father Luc's bushy eyebrows fused into one as he squinted. "You fence, I assume?"

"Of course. I'd be honoured to spar with you, if that's still part of your protocol."

Father Luc pointed to a long white scar that ran across his palm, from his pinky to below the thumb. "This injury was one of the hardest to heal. Be careful of feet and hands."

Athos moved on to the next blade, noting the priest hadn't said yes to a match.

"This sword seems perfect. A keepsake?" Athos wielded it into the *engarde* position.

Father Luc shook his head and walked to the other side of the table, where he appeared to command a pulpit, his hands on his front as if it were a dais. "I would counsel you to lay down arms and favour a life of devotion or academics."

Athos muffled a snicker and picked up two swords, one in each hand. "Why keep these then?"

"To remind me my life as a Musketeer is over." The priest stood dead still.

The sword in Athos's dominant hand was the essence of beauty and power. Its weight suited his muscles, and he be-came spellbound by the shine, turning it over several times to study its qualities. If he loved anything more than women or poetry, it was a good weapon. "You don't expect me to take your advice."

"From what I can see," Father Luc's mouth turned down, "you'll need much more convincing."

Athos returned the swords to their lineup and walked the length of the table once and back. A duel, a siege, a headstrong argument, most of the swords had likely drawn blood. Getting the priest to open up about their mysteries might prove tricky. "I must protect myself from looking vulnerable," Athos argued, expecting no sympathy. "If poverty or a bad crop were to strike my lands, fighting is the only defence of my title. I'm stronger knowing the sword."

"Sometimes threats don't come from violent men."

Athos moved to the end of the table. "Why did you quit? Did you lose your nerve?"

Father Luc's frown changed to placid contemplation. "I nearly lost my life several times. God intervened."

"You could teach me skills I have yet to learn. I'm good with a sword but untested."

"You and a hundred other men of your kind," the priest countered and sighed. "Don't think I'm deaf to your request or the logic behind it. But you won't find God at the tip of a sword."

Athos approached him, and they stood face-to-face. "It's not against the church to teach me a different kind of devotion, as you put it. Consider yourself a spiritual adviser for a greater good."

Father Luc's belly shook before a laugh bubbled out of his mouth; all the while, his head ticked back and forth. "You mistake me for a warrior. You'd be better off bribing the

church for political survival, but don't tell anyone I said that."
His laugh died to a grumble.

Athos dropped his gaze to the swords, laid out like hash marks of glory.

"My best use to you," the priest said, "is for your religious needs. Your reputation is that you are a man devoted to his faith."

"I try to live by the church's teachings, less successfully than some would like."

"You mean Father Turre's expectations? Your father's?"

"No," Athos said, rubbing hands together. "My own."

"You disappoint yourself? That's quite an admission. By what standard?"

"I need to marry and put aside youthful urges." Athos checked to see the priest's reaction, which was one of acceptance.

"Marital issues can be problematic, but you have control over your own destiny, more so than most men. You can pick any wife you want. Nothing prevents you from finding a match sooner or later." The priest squinted. "But you're lost, I can see. Tell me why."

"My heart." Athos flinched at the priest's next burst of laughter, which lasted longer than usual but clipped to an end once Athos didn't join in.

"You want to love the woman you marry? Here are my first words of absolute truth. Love is thoroughly unnecessary. God forgive me—," the priest looked up, "—but a sovereign's wife is simply a necessity to perpetuate your bloodline. I'm not telling you anything you don't already know, Athos."

Athos spun away from Father Luc and placed one foot after the other, not knowing which direction to go, like his recent interactions with Anne. He wished he hadn't been so candid about love. The priest came up behind him and placed a hand on his shoulder before Athos arrived at the door.

"Let me redirect," Father Luc said. "I'm here as a resource. Tell me what you need, and I'll do better to hold back my incessant chuckles."

•   •   •

Athos took Father Luc to the library to gain some distance from the allure of the swords. Though he had gotten off to a wobbly start, Athos began to tell his story of meeting Anne. Partly due to the quiet of the library and also due to his recent lack of friends to confide in, Athos's story turned into a total confession. He recounted the nymphs at Agape Lake, the cat in the confessional cupboard, the honey house, until there wasn't an unclean act or thought that his new confessor did not know about. Confession always made Athos feel much better, as if a bright light on a dark spot turned it pure again.

What he hadn't expected was his heart to start growing. He was becoming attached to Anne—her beauty, her intellect, her animalism—and these thoughts tumbled out with emotional abandon.

"My, my," Father Luc said after crossing himself. He closed his eyes and bowed his head into prayerful hands. Athos knew the priest might dole out a penance to top any previously issued by Father Turre. "I absolutely do not condone your behaviour at the monastery. Or any of it, for that matter."

"Of course not," Athos said, his heart sinking a little.

"But," Father Luc went on, "I do see merit in your resistance of this young woman's charms. You need spiritual reinforcement. Your will has been tested, but you also recognise God working in your life, which is good."

"Should I marry her?" Athos had also asked God the same question, but perhaps the priest could interpret. "I still know so little about her."

"You cannot continue to compromise yourself *and her* as you have been."

Athos rose from their place in the armchairs near the large window, where the sunlight was slipping into grey. "Then I have no choice."

Father Luc came to stand behind him. "It would be my pleasure to meet the future wife of the Comte de la Fere."

They stood silently for a while, watching the day fall into darkness, then Father Luc doled out a penance to Athos, which involved many hours alone on his knees with a rosary.

# 13

# Meeting Anne

Athos arranged for a meeting between Father Luc and Anne the following week at the cathedral in Blois. Athos had sent her a written invitation on his heaviest stationery. Writing it did little to reinforce his state of penitence. It had the opposite effect. The curls of his script induced images her bare curves underneath him in the honey house. Fantasies trailed him the whole week like a constant spring rain. He resorted to taking the pillow book to bed one night to relieve his pent-up desire, something he hadn't done in years.

The day for the meeting came before he'd heard back from Anne. It didn't change his plans. He knew it was her way. Athos arrived at the door of the church wearing his finest embroidered doublet. Father Luc played the part by dressing in formal robes. Upon first glance at each other, they broke into laughter.

"We're outfitted for the Queen," Father Luc chortled.

"Just wait," Athos said in a sarcastic tone.

Father Luc escorted Athos to his study, formerly Turre's, and offered a pear slice from a wooden cutting board. A series of pre-marital instructions between a potential bride and groom was required with a priest, although Athos felt that formality was premature. This meeting was a test of her suitability for him, and the enormity of today's event was palpable. Athos remembered asking his father once what their priest had thought of mother. He answered, "Adequate."

Anne was not adequate. He sweated over the reality—she was the embodiment of sensuality. He shuddered at the potential disaster to his matrimonial prospects.

A whoosh of air from the door to the priest's study refocused Athos on the task at hand. Anne stood outlined in light, wearing a shimmering gown of two shades of beige. The accent colour at her collar and sleeves was red and set off her swept-up blond hair, which rivalled the gold of Midas. Athos needed to shake his head, but thought better of it.

Before Athos could offer an introduction, she was bowing at Father Luc's fingertips, using a feather-light grasp.

"Father Luc," she said, a notch above a whisper. She glanced to Athos. In the arrow of her blue eyes, he quickly closed his mouth.

"Mademoiselle de Breuil," Father Luc returned. He tipped his head and offered a seat, one of two in front of his desk. "It's an honour to meet you."

She took her seat, snagging a slice of pear as she sat, and nibbled on the skin. Enrapt, Athos hesitated to sit until Father Luc shot an impatient glance at him. Athos was silently thanking God that her dress covered her bosom.

"Anne," Athos sputtered out before sitting, "thank you for coming."

"Your company is most desirable," she said. Her smile matched the warmth growing in Athos middle section and lower. He redirected his thoughts to pruning roses.

After a long pause, Athos said, "Father Luc is the new priest at my church. I spoke of you and he asked for us to meet."

"Is it true you were a Musketeer?"

At her question, Father Luc craned his neck as if a crick had developed. "I haven't fought for His Majesty in two seasons. Once I took orders, I laid my swords to rest."

"But I understand you have a fine collection of weapons under Fere's care."

Athos couldn't grasp how she knew. He decided to corner each servant later to find the gossiper.

"I don't consider them possessions," the priest said, "as much as relics of a past life."

She nodded and bit her pear slice in two. She chewed and grinned in a way that suggested she was forming another thought. Both Athos and Father Luc leaned in slightly to hear it.

*She already has my priest under her spell.*

"I brought you a gift for your arrival." Anne reached into a matching beige clutch and placed a gleaming jar of honey on Father Luc's desk. "I hope you like honey."

Father Luc coughed into his dark sleeve and tried to work up a smile. He was unable to resist a quick look at Athos. Though he was not as surprised, Athos was struggling to remember the Latin term for daisy or tulip, any item in nature other than honey or honeysuckle.

"Thank you," Father Luc finally managed and placed the jar inside a top desk drawer. He clapped it shut. "Athos tells me you favour poetry."

"He's kind." She held her blue-eyed gaze onto Athos's flushed face two seconds too long. She slipped the last of the pear between her lips. "Actually, I not only favour poetry, I love it."

Athos nodded and strained for a comfortable, but discrete, position in his seat. "She brought me a book from an English poet whom the French haven't discovered. Shakespeare. I hate to admit it, but he's a master at sonnets."

"Sonnets about the fierceness of love," Anne corrected.

"And your brother? Is he also a man of letters?" Father Luc asked. "I didn't meet him in Paris at the church. Nor did I meet anyone who knew him."

"You will meet." Anne straightened against the seatback and checked the buttons on her sleeves, each fastened tightly. "Do you read poetry, Father Luc?"

"I read inspired texts on religion. Some on natural sciences," Father Luc said, gesturing toward a stout bookshelf behind him. "I'm afraid my reading trends toward the more concrete rather than the abstract."

"But what could be more inspired than a poetic phrase about the human condition?" She seemed to challenge Father Luc, but in a cool way. "Poetry is inspired. I'd argue that it's divinely inspired."

"The Bible is the first inspired text," Father Luc said, his face shining with sincere curiosity at the direction of the conversation.

Athos's heart drummed loudly inside his ribs. "Anne favours the Greek poets."

"I favour anything that pleases me," she said and smoothed an eyebrow and tucked a lock of hair behind her ear in one lush move.

Tamping down another unwelcome urge between his legs, Athos groped for less suggestive words.

"She favours words that touch the heart," Athos offered, shifting his weight.

Anne rose to the bookshelf behind the priest. She entwined a stray curl of her hair in her finger, released it, then ran her hand down the spine of a thick grey book. "Words are beauty immortalised."

Neither of the men spoke. Athos's tongue thickened, useless. Father Luc's deep breathing was the only sound in the stuffy room. Anne's eyes fluttered, inviting a response from the two statues staring in her direction.

Father Luc rubbed his chin, opened his mouth, and immediately closed it. He reached for a small palm-sized notepad and quill. He flipped to a page, past several sheets full of notes. "And how has your brother's reception been? What sense do you have of his settling into his role?"

Anne floated back to her chair with a book and sat. She tightened one hand into a fist, which she hid under the book. "He's finding his way."

"He's stepped into his role easily," Athos followed up, watching to see if her hand would relax, unlike the knot below his waistline, which could have used a good book for cover. "To his credit, he appears confident in the pulpit."

"And you two," Father Luc said and eyed them both, "appear comfortable with each other."

"As I said," Anne said, uncurling her fist and offering the book to Athos with a knowing nod, "I favour anything that pleases me."

Athos laid the book on his lap, choked back a whimper, and crossed his legs.

Writing again, Father Luc made a flourish with the quill. "Please send my greetings to your brother," he said and ripped the sheet from his notebook to hand across the desk, "and assure him I will try my best to visit or arrange a meeting soon."

She tucked the folded note into her clutch and pursed her lips. "He's quite busy."

Father Luc began writing on a second page. "Now, as for the two of you—"

"Father Luc," Anne interrupted. He paused his quill and nodded *go ahead*. "In your study of natural sciences, do you see connections between Biblical passages and the condition of men and women?"

The priest wrinkled his forehead. Athos couldn't tell if he was taken aback or intrigued. He hoped the latter.

"The Bible is mostly about the human condition. Be more specific," Father Luc said.

"From my study of important treatises," Anne began, poised as if a nun presenting catechism, "our love of God begins with the love of another. Man loves the Creator when he learns to love mankind." She titled her head. "Or a woman."

Father Luc repositioned himself in his chair. "You have it turned around. We must love God, first and foremost, before we can know the love of another. Everything emanates from our love of God."

Unfazed and eyes shining, she volleyed. "True, God is love and man is the image of God. Therefore, doesn't it make sense that love—from a man, of course," she clasped her hands, "—is the essence of God himself?"

Athos pressed the book into his lap and tried to memorise her last words. God, man, love. He cherished the sound of them coming from her throat.

But from the looks of Father Luc, the same wasn't true. The priest had dulled the end of the quill from pressing down too hard.

"You and your brother must have some interesting debates," Father Luc said before he laid the feather into the notebook and closed it. "Have you spent time in a convent, my lady?" There was a strain in the priest's voice that Athos hadn't heard before.

Athos intervened. "She grew up among men studying for the priesthood," he cast her a quick smile, "so she has had many years to debate the finer points of modern theology."

"Yes, well," Father Luc hesitated, "what you may call modern might be described by some as sacrilegious."

"But love is not sacrilegious." She wasn't backing down. On the contrary, Athos watched her edge forward, appearing to sharpen her argument behind calculating eyes. "It's beautiful. God's creation. Man's delight."

The muscles in Father Luc's jaw flexed. Athos had rarely seen a man of God so flustered. The priest's eyes hardened, his hands flattened on the desk, and his cheeks fought a frown. From the looks of him, Father Luc was pushing down a heavy-handed preaching. Or worse.

"Father Luc," Athos said, scooting his chair closer into the brewing storm, careful to keep the book lap-bound. "Do you mind if Anne has a look at your sword collection?"

The debaters stopped preparing thunderbolts and threw their attention toward him. In a snap, the room grew a little less muggy. He thought he heard a muted sigh of pleasure spill out of Anne at the suggestion. When their eyes met, she gobbled him from top to bottom, lingering a few seconds at the book.

"A woman and swords." Father Luc sighed, too. He mustered a weak grin and leaned back into his chair though not all the way. "I guess in this case, that's not unusual."

"It would be an honour," Anne said, rising. "But you must excuse me and save the swords for another day. I have an important errand, so I must say *adieu*." She stood half outside the study door before they could comprehend her departure. She briefly turned back to Athos before leaving. "I think you'll enjoy that book."

Clumsily, Athos stood up, his back to the priest, and the book dropped from his lap. Rounding the desk, Father Luc picked it up and glanced at the title before showing it to Athos, who read it and sprang for the door. *Beekeeping: The Intricacies of Making Honey.*

•   •   •

Athos dashed through the church to reach Anne before she left.

"I believe I owe you an apology," he said, his hand lightly covering hers on the wrought-iron handle of the front door.

"For what?" Mischievousness oozed from her reply as she turned to him. Her question hung between their lips.

"For our encounter at the monastery. Will you forgive me for being so forward?" *What am I saying? She invites all my wantonness. But she deserves my best self.* He had not planned on having this conversation. In fact, he wasn't sure why he felt an apology was necessary, except for an overwhelming need in him to aim higher.

*But her lips, so close.*

"My Fere." She turned her hand from the door to entwine his fingers. "Your forwardness is all I think about."

Leaning in slowly, she touched his lips. Not a full kiss. A tease. A taste.

A moan lay in his chest waiting, like the rest of his hunger.

"Must you leave?" An inadequate response. His real desire was to say: *Take me. Take me with you.*

"Fere, what is it you want most from me?" Her question, like her body heat, stirred his manhood.

"Besides Eden?" he teased back, desirous of a full kiss. Then he grew serious. His intentions demanded seriousness. "I want you to be vulnerable to me. And not just your body. All of you. Your mind, Anne. I want to know your mind."

The craving, like none he'd ever known, was out in the open. He liked it. Pushed it. "I want to be sated by every part of you."

Her sly shield, the playfulness she always wore, her ability to evade and deflect, seemed to wane. He gathered her in his arms, and he physically felt the barrier drop. It was an anchor in his embrace. For the first time, he relished that he was feeling and seeing a new side of her.

She drew in a shaky breath and turned her cheek to his wanting lips. "I ... I'm touched." Her heart seemed to be speaking out of turn, but not for long. "I must go."

As if a cat wriggling from capture, she slipped from his arms, out the door, and left him empty-handed. Starving.

The door creaked to a close, and a minute passed before Father Luc tapped his shoulder. When Athos finally turned, the priest sucked in his cheeks.

"She regrets the shortness of her visit," Athos said, backing away from the priest's withering gaze.

Arms behind his back, Father Luc faced the sanctuary. "My impression of her isn't a good one."

Athos slumped, a mirror opposite of the priest's stance. The crucifix in the altar burned in Athos's eyes, and he could see the outline of the cross even when he closed his lids. "Yes. She's bold, but from what I've discovered, it's been her defence for survival."

"What *do* you know of her?"

Athos heard no judgment in the query. "She's an orphan who suffered and endured untold personal humiliation, which she didn't deserve."

"And?"

"And what?" Athos looked at Father Luc's profile, pronounced by a backdrop of stained glass.

"Who is she? Who is her family? Where does she come from? Who can vouch for her?" He paused. "Other than her brother."

Athos took two steps forward. *Does it matter?* It didn't to him. Not anymore. He found his authoritative sovereign voice. "Her brother is a priest, and from what I can judge, a learned and serious man."

"Whom no one in my circles has ever met." Father Luc cleared phlegm from the back of his throat. "You'll have to excuse my bluntness, but my quick inquiries in Paris about him uncovered very little."

"More than likely because he originally came from England, although they're French," Athos countered, growing irritated. "*Someone* assigned him his parish."

"Yes, Cardinal Richelieu. Not necessarily the King's most loyal subject."

"A quick assessment is, as you put it, *quick*. I'd encourage you to reserve judgment on their family before you've met them all."

Father Luc turned Athos toward him by the elbow. "Right now, it would be imprudent of me to bless a union between the two of you."

Athos tried filling his chest, behind which lay a dull ache. "I anticipated your displeasure. But I had hoped you wouldn't dismiss her after only one meeting."

"You're clouded. You need clarity."

"About what? Every nuance of her past? No one ever knows a person through and through, not even you of God."

"God may be a mystery, but He's also an open book," Father Luc said, uplifting his eyes to Heaven. "Your position requires a greater degree of discretion. Certainly a wife is necessary, but an ill-chosen wife is a liability."

Athos tucked his chin and rubbed his eyes. At times like these, he wanted his father's advice. More deeply, he wanted God's. "And if I choose not to give her up yet?"

"Are you in love with her?" The priest asked in a reedy voice.

"A few days ago you were counselling me that love didn't matter. All I need is a wife, you said. An heir. Any woman would do. If all Anne lacks is your approval, I believe you're imposing a double standard."

"It's not what she lacks that I'm afraid of," he said, walking past him toward the direction of the study. "It's what she has too much of."

Father Luc came to the first row of pews and stood still. "I appreciate your honourable intentions, Athos. But I advise you to consider this union carefully—with your heart *and* your mind." He turned and pointed directly between Athos's eyes. "And not because of other parts of your body."

Athos stayed behind and fell into the hard pew, thankful that the priest had not pointed between his legs.

# An Unintended Triangle

The night of the failed interview, Athos dreamt of Eden. He was alone, nude, seeing the garden for the first time. Lilacs on trellises and butterfly bushes filled the air with their aromas. Grape vines burst with bundles of every colour of grape imaginable. The grass under his bare feet was as soft as goose down. In the sky, the blue after a spring rain, birds frolicked close above his head and rabbits zipped across his path, in the direction of the Tree of Knowledge.

The Tree grew in a grove full of lesser trees. Nothing marked the way to this statuesque centre point in the garden. Nothing needed to. By instinct, Athos walked into the sacred territory of its wide canopy. The tree embodied the kernel of first light, a generative glow. It represented the warmth of his mother. The strength of his father. A vessel of truth.

Athos circled around the inner rim of the canopy and spiraled slowly inward toward the trunk. Every step closer increased his desire for the fruit hanging from the limbs. Ripe, red apples. Their aroma made his stomach hunger. Yet he abstained and walked in a circle until he could touch the coarse bark and absorb the energy of the tree's power at its strongest.

The reverence of this connection turned his heart inside out. He felt a knowing and an opening. He knew the tree contained knowledge of every wonderful and base human trait. The tree could also read his soul and saw the wonder and flaws in him.

He sat at its base on an exposed root and leaned back to look up. The wind curled the leaves and fluttered his hair. The apples tottered back and forth and one dropped within a few feet of his reach. He wanted to grab it and devour its secrets. The urge rushed through his blood and weakened his willpower. Thinking a touch would be enough, he leaned toward it, and the grass beneath the apple moved. The head of a snake rose from underneath the ripe temptation.

Athos's first instinct was to speak. He believed the snake would understand, would agree to a taste. Instead, the serpent snapped and pierced Athos in the soft flap of skin between the thumb and forefinger. He flinched backward. He rubbed the puncture wounds and folded himself protectively inward. Looking back at the apple, Athos watched the snake disappear.

The bite throbbed and his hand began to redden. He rubbed the sore and his body grew cold. Trembling, Athos blew warm air on his hands but the hurt deepened and the stinging venom moved up his arm and into his shoulders, creeping along his nerves until it pricked the base of his scalp. It stung and dulled at the same time. He panted in fear, afraid that the snake was an agent of the Devil, who would take him below the earth. The apple, he thought, might save his life. Shaken, he lunged for the fallen fruit and bit it the moment the snake's poison blinded him. His body fell limp on the bed of grass and the canopy closed around him.

•   •   •

Athos woke up in a clammy state, sheets damp, his hair stuck to his forehead and nape. He rose, dressed in loose lounging pants and took a lit candle downstairs to the library through the secret passage from his bedroom. From the leaded window, the light of dawn allowed him to write a letter, a means of sorting through the dream.

The images were a warning. Father Luc's hesitation about Anne was warranted. She was the temptress and the temptation, the snake *and* the apple. A sinful promise of worldly delight and fulfilment. His dream clarified his dilemma—he did not possess the self-control to go alone on his quest to win her honourably. He needed help.

*Demi.*

With Bronte gone, Demi was the closest friend he had. And in some ways, she was the better of the two in this endeavour. Of his friends, she was the most level-headed and calm, traits he needed to stay chaste. The drawback was that Demi was a woman with high standards, who might scoff at being his and Anne's chaperon.

A correct assumption, he found out, when he met Demi to discuss the idea.

"You want me to do what?" Demi shot up from the pew at the cathedral. Athos caught her gently by the elbow and guided her back down. The only impression Demi had of Anne was her naked dip in Agape Lake, the event that almost ruined Bronte's marriage proposal.

"I don't think asking you to befriend Anne and be our companion is an outlandish proposal," Athos said, though he struggled to sound convincing.

"Excuse me while I try to find a teardrop of empathy," she said, patting her red face with a handkerchief. "Her brazen behaviour—or what I've seen of it—is sinful." She pleaded with her doe-like brown eyes. "Why, Athos? Why are you drawn to her?"

He looked away, at the ornate carvings on the balustrade, grasping for a rational response. "I can't explain my attraction to her, Demi. It's the same with you and Bronte. To put it kindly, he's a rascal whose behaviour is questionable at times. Yet, you love him."

"Do you love her?" Demi knotted her handkerchief.

He shook his head, the truth eluding him. "How do you explain love?"

Worry lines creased her forehead, and Demi untwisted the handkerchief over her lap. "I hoped you'd sent your note because you'd heard from him. I can hardly breathe not knowing where he is or the day he'll return, regardless of Margot."

Athos slipped an arm around her shoulders and took the handkerchief. He smoothed it out across his thigh. "Bronte is lucky. You love him without judgment." His hand slipped into hers, which had continued to fidget across the puff of her skirt.

"If," she said, reiterating, "*if* I choose to help you, I won't be dishonest. I'll agree to meet her and decide for myself if it's even possible for me to act as a buffer. Oh, Athos! From what you've told me, she won't like me being around."

An understatement. For Demi's sake, or so he'd rationalised, Athos had chosen to describe Anne as less bold. He'd glossed over their sins, depicting them as stolen kisses and inappropriate touches. He left out details about the honey house and Father Luc's disapproval of Anne. Selfishly, he knew the real story would quash his plan.

"Athos?" she asked as she sunk into his side. "Why have we chosen to love people who challenge us?"

He tossed a smile of resignation at her, and she at him. He felt an irresistible urge to touch her cheek. Her face harboured no secrets, in contrast to Anne's, but the sweet piety of his gesture grew into a deeper, less platonic feeling the longer his hand lingered. Demi's smile faded, and he felt a tinge of remorse for being so familiar, for feeling something he shouldn't feel for a woman in love with another man. His best friend.

Unable to resist, his fingers brushed her lips. She closed her eyes and kissed his fingertips, and he moved into her.

Stunned by the warmth of her lips on his, he was reluctant to stop. Unwillingly, he drew back, knowing this was a place they both couldn't stay in. He studied her expression, full of want and pain. He touched her cheek again and fought to think of a rational explanation.

"Demi." His whisper was too husky to come off as regretful. "We're both vulnerable right now. Let's not complicate our lives further." But unwisely, he wanted another kiss. He knew it was possible from the look in her eyes. So he followed impurity to its conclusion.

The second kiss was stronger. Less irrational, more fateful, to release the pent-up force between them that had been building for years without an outlet. They had crossed a defenceless boundary.

Demi broke contact and slid away in the pew, burying her face in her hands. He understood not to touch her again. "You know I love you, too," he said. "We're as close as any friends can be. We must forgive each other. We're just in need of reassurance right now."

She nodded and softly cried into her palms. He clenched his own, fighting back an embrace.

His rational self could explain the mistake; his heart could not. He did not protest her quick departure. The church became a tomb, and he folded her handkerchief and buried it in his pocket.

# Athos's Log, Undated

*My spirit is restless. Every turn is a blind corridor, where I come upon a dark presence. My friendships have dissolved and my mind cannot sleep. She invades my thoughts. She and she. Who will dominate my heart and mind?*

# 15

# A Duel of Wits and Fortitude

A week passed, and Demi stayed away. Equally troubling, no word arrived from Bronte. Athos's world grew smaller and smaller.

At the end of the week, following a sombre service by Father Luc on the topic of long suffering, Athos rode to Averdon to find Anne. Unannounced, he entered her brother's church to search for her.

Music inside the nave covered the sound of the door. With his back to Athos, Father de Breuil faced the organ in the choir area and played a short hymn, one-handed. Then repeated. Anne stood behind him, off-centre, listening and humming along to each stanza. This was the first time Athos had seen brother and sister together.

She twisted loose curls from her hair, swept up in combs. The habit suggested volumes about her. Hers wasn't a nervous habit, Athos deduced, because rather than make her tense, it relaxed her. The tightening, then the loosening. Again, again, which caused her shoulders to drop and her back to curve. A tension and release. A little like her interactions with him. She was both fuse and spark, and when the fireworks ended, satisfaction reigned. At least, he hoped it would.

Keeping quiet, Athos hung back while brother and sister let down their guards. She hummed and twisted curls; the priest nodded and played along. They were at ease. No formalities distanced them. Her hand dropped to the back of her brother's nape. He continued to play and to roll his head from side to side as she stroked his neck below the hairline.

At a distance, the act seemed innocent, a gentle hand on a sore spot. Athos came closer while Anne continued to caress and squeeze her brother's shoulders. The priest lifted his face up to her, and she lightly stroked his cheek. The hair on Athos's neck spiked.

"Father de Breuil," Athos involuntarily blurted the name to breath again.

"Monsieur," the priest bolted upright, "you surprise us." He abandoned his sister by the bench and walked steadily toward Athos, who thought the priest's calm looked practised.

Staying behind, Anne tucked a stray lock of hair into the loose bundle behind her head. Rather than appear surprised, she stretched out a hand to beckon Athos forward.

He felt at odds with his instincts, a feeling that whatever he had just seen might have been more than he could explain. At the least, Anne's soft touches confirmed everything he thought about her. She loved being physical. If he replayed the moment in his mind, would it look more like an act of loving kindness or something more? Maybe, he was on the brink of insanity. Who in their right mind would believe him?

"I'm pleased to see you, Monsieur," the priest said, glancing back at his sister. "We both are."

"You two seem very close." Athos wasn't looking at the priest, wasn't asking him, wasn't sure he wanted any sort of answer.

"We've had to rely on each other for many years," Anne said. Her smile made his heart double its pace.

"I hear your meeting with Father Luc went well, yes?" Father de Breuil asked.

"Went well?" Athos finally shook himself to comprehend the statement. *Is the world upside down?* "You spoke with Father Luc?"

"Why, yes. Two days ago," de Breuil said.

Feeling left out, Athos played along. "And Anne, did you speak with him again?"

"I did," she said, glowing with pleasure. "I showed him my book of Shakespeare."

"Ah," was all Athos could fumble out. Another blind corridor. They were everywhere.

"Shall we read?" Anne asked, coming near. "You asked me to read to you and we haven't."

The brother stepped aside and Anne took his place.

"Are you up for it today?" she asked.

Athos never played well at pretend games. He couldn't hide his deeper emotions. He nodded, and asked the priest, "May I have her?"

The clergyman's eyes and mouth formed a too-perfect smile. "By all means." The whoosh of his retreating robes filled the silence. Athos's neck relaxed, and he bowed.

•   •   •

Athos escorted Anne to an apple grove behind the church. The canopy shaded them from the noon-day heat and the trees provided a modicum of privacy. Anne tried holding his hand, but he avoided it until he suggested a place to sit, on a flat area covered with moss. He kicked a few fallen apples from the spot and laid out his doublet for her. Her forehead wrinkled at the small courtesy, a subtle sign of wariness. He hadn't said a word outside.

He positioned himself to sit in front of her on the grass, but not at a convenient reach. He resisted using an anvil to break the ice. "I want you to tell me more about yourself."

"Like why my brother and I are so close?"

The spike shattered the cold.

"Well, it appears a little more than 'close.'"

"If I may," she said, twirling a curl, "an outsider might think the same of you and Bronte."

Before he could respond—not that a comprehensible comeback was forthcoming—she continued. "Even the King is rumoured to cultivate close relationships with several dukes." She sighed. "My brother and I had to cope. Maybe I was wrong to share our story with you."

She tucked her legs beneath her dress and leaned her head back to peer into the shade.

"You have one of the keenest minds I've ever known," he said, both wishing it weren't so and envying her sharpness.

"And what it tells me is that people live many lives other than the ones they reveal to others." She inclined toward him so that her cleavage became the feature. "I believe I know something about you."

And about every man, he thought in a slight stupor. She wanted him to lose his wits. Instead, he baited her. He leaned toward her bosom until his lips all but touched the delicate cleavage.

"What you may not know about me," he said, inhaling her scent, "is that I have recovered my self-control."

As predictable as a cat startled by a loud noise, she tossed him back from her milky flesh and simmered, her mouth a straight line.

He laughed, finally letting the tension of the strangeness between them dissipate. Her feet fluttered in aggravation beneath her dress.

"Oh please," he urged, faking a pout.

She huffed, crossed her hands over her chest, looked over her far shoulder, and jutted out her chin. He tried to turn her face back in his direction. She pretended to bite his fingers. He ruefully shook his hand as if she had snapped it.

"I often think of you," he said, "as pure feline."

She raised her chin an inch more.

"I like cats," he said. He reached for an apple lying nearby in the moss, brushed it off, and tossed it into her lap. She flinched, but her frown faded to mild aggravation. She threw the apple over her shoulder. His laughter eventually loosened her stern stare and the last vestiges of his doubt.

He uncurled her crossed arms and laid her hand over the top of his fingers. She didn't stop him. Porcelain and smooth, her hand covered his rough spots.

"What are we about?" he asked, stroking the back of her hand.

"You and I? Or God's plan for the world?"

He felt a slight stiffness in her hand lessen. "Us," he said, nodding to her. "I'm trying to sort us out using my brain rather than other parts of me."

She began to return his caresses on the top of his hand as she reclined on one elbow. "Your brain is your pleasure centre. It triggers your body."

"Poetry gives us mutual, platonic pleasure," he said, pleased that she continued to pet him.

"Then we should read it every hour." Turning onto her stomach, she hugged her top half so that her breasts plumped into an irresistible showcase. He averted his gaze and plucked a fresh apple from the closest low-hanging limb. Taking a large bite, the juice dripped down his chin. The sweetness waylaid his other hunger.

"Who taught you to read poetry?" he said, placing the apple within reach of her mouth.

She nipped at a dangling bite. "Gregori."

He wished he hadn't asked. "Have you ever been separated from him?"

Her gaze drifted into the distance as if she focused on something private. "Never."

"The sonnets seem suited for passion rather than piety," he ventured.

"As for Shakespeare," she said, back from her moment, "I forgot the book."

He shook his head and sighed. Her ruse made him think of Father Luc, whom she'd visited without his knowledge.

"Anne," he said, appreciating the way her eyes widened at his attention, "the day you spoke with Father Luc, did you speak of me?"

"Do you mean, did he tell me he disapproved of our marriage?"

Athos choked down an apple chunk.

She rolled on her back. From upside down, her cleavage was just as luscious. "We spoke," she said, "about poetry and religious doctrine and how he would not marry us. At least, not now."

"You spent that much time with him?" He took another bite, thinking while chewing. If all she said were true, Father Luc might know more about Anne than he did. "You don't seem upset by his refusal."

She snipped a sprig of clover from the moss and slipped it between her breasts and gazed into the tree canopy. "Why should I be?"

"For obvious reasons."

"Because you won't make love to me until we marry?" She smiled back at him, tilting her head so that she wasn't staring at him upside down. "There's more to sensuality than simply our bodies, Fere."

His tongue refused to speak.

"Fere?" She spun over and posed like a cat on the prowl. "You do know there's more to mutual oblivion than my body against yours?"

He wanted to know. He wanted to be taught.

"You know it already," she said, slinking toward him on all fours. "Your words, Fere. Your words are intoxicants."

Athos's tongue unwound. "*Love's fire heats water. Water cools not love.*"

"I love that you've memorised Shakespeare's good lines," she said, still stalking him.

"Listen to my heart," he said and placed her nearest hand on his chest for several beats, staring into her sharp blue eyes. "My heart is true, Anne. I seek love. When I see you, you stir my blood."

"And more." She leaned in for a kiss. He leaned away.

"So much more," he said. He grazed her cheek with his knuckles. "*On thy beauty, I will alight. For thy love, I will fight. Against thy breast, I will be still. Forsaking the end and—*"

"*—and God's will,*" she completed. "Your poem. It brought me to you."

He kissed her earlobe. She rubbed his neck. "We can marry soon," she whispered, "if you wish."

"Not without Father Luc's—"

"My brother will marry us, Fere."

He backed off from her neckline and studied her eyes. Her hopefulness opened the door of possibility and trouble. "He's your brother, not my priest. To ask him to conduct the Mass instead of Father Luc would be a side-step, a rebuke."

"And a sovereign's right to his own happiness," she interjected, clutching his shoulders. "You're the law in this province. *You* decide who marries and who doesn't. This includes *you.*"

"It could make Father Luc my adversary. I need allies," he said, suddenly standing and pulling her up by the waist. "Without Bronte, I have few."

"I am your ally." She nudged him with her shoulder and stood on her own accord. He noticed the clover had flattened between her white breasts.

"You deserve love," he said and gathered her in his arms, "as much as Eve."

"So you'll allow Gregori to marry us?"

"I'll make a decision once Bronte returns," he answered.

Her eyes turned cold. "Bronte isn't your keeper."

"But he's my closest friend."

"And if he says no?" Her back girdled against his embrace.

"You," he said, studying one eye then the other for thawing, "will have to wait until he returns to get an answer."

She wiggled to get free. He held her tighter.

"I am not an *either-or*, Fere. I am an *all*."

He loosened his hold, and she teetered backward until she stood at arm's distance.

"By God's oath, I choose all," he said and grabbed another apple from a low branch and offered it to her.

She refused it. "You will *forsake* God to choose me. Your poem declares it."

"So it does, figuratively," he said with a single nod. "Your hand, please."

She opened her palm.

He placed the apple in it. "I give you my word. We will marry and know the ways of love."

Her shell cracked, by the width of a thin line, enough for him to seize a quick kiss. Then he tugged her by the hand back to the door of the church, leaving her with a promise.

"I have a token of my intentions for you," he said. "Meet me at the lake tomorrow so I can present it to you properly."

# 16

# And God Created Woman

Athos kept his mother's ring in a small casket of important family treasures at Valliere. His father had handed over the key to the lockbox a week before death had overtaken him.

"My son." His father's cold hand had clamped around Athos's wrist. A clock chimed twice in the dark bedroom suite, where his father's spirit had flickered and finally succumbed. "Rule this land with your head. Be fair. Be honest. Let the province be your refuge from the ills of Paris. Those who want to undermine you there cannot penetrate your authority here unless you harbour the poison of doubt."

For the first time since his father's death, Athos took the casket's key from a high shelf in the library and discovered he didn't needed it. The lock on the oblong box was broken.

The iron hinges creaked open. Athos knew the contents by heart—significant gold and silver heirlooms of jewellery, provincial maps, records of his lineage—except he had felt few urges to open it after burying his father. Today, he retrieved his mother's sapphire ring.

He fished it out of a small velvet pouch and rubbed the plush side of the fabric across the facets. The stone glimmered. He couldn't remember the ring on his mother's finger, but it must have declared her to be a figure of regal importance. As it would Anne.

The morning crawled by though he relented to spending it on neglected requests for his time. He agreed to an audience with a long line of men in the province, farmers, guildsmen and merchants, who brought a litany of worries and requests pertaining to crop yields and livestock, taxes and rents. Dull in comparison to the events he would set in motion that afternoon. The promise of his own matrimony.

Athos kept the ring in his pocket throughout the litany of visitors, then later he carried it from room to room in the estate, surveying the layout and wondering how it would feel after Anne lived with him, in charge of the estate's social life, which he had ignored too long. Courtiers he needed to please politically would find a welcome table at Valliere, plus ample amounts of wine and a wickedly charming hostess, the Comtesse de la Fere.

At exactly noon, Athos arrived at the banks of Agape Lake, in the now notorious spot where he had first seen Anne naked, except for the black tag on her arm. He smiled a little at the memory. Soon, she would be all his.

After he'd spent fifteen minutes of waiting in the heat, Anne sneaked up from behind and covered his mouth with her hands. He tensed at the surprise, disappointed that his guard had been down due to the mesmerising water, but he mellowed into her breathing and softness.

"Shh," she whispered on the back of his neck. "Do you promise to be quiet?"

He nodded, and she dropped her hands from his lips, which now tasted of her sweet aroma. Down his shoulders, arms, hips, thighs, her hands memorised his outline. His blood grew denser.

Coming around into his line of sight, she held a finger up to her lips and backed toward the water's edge. Her hair undone, she wore a see-through shift, under which the dark roses of her nipples blazed. Fleetingly, he wondered how she could have ridden to the lake without arousing every peasant along the way. Even the women.

He started to say her name, but she shook her head and smiled. "Patience," she urged.

The moving water snagged the edge of her garment and soaked the hem. The weight pulled the fabric down in front and hugged her breasts, pronouncing the red blossoms. He started for her and as he did, she began to gather up the sheer fabric. First above her ankles, then above her knees, to the soft blond patch between her legs.

*Land of Eden. Field of bliss.*

Halting, he fixated there as she rocked her hips slightly from side to side, her thighs the tinder. She continued to undress and paused before each reveal. At hips. Navel. Her torso. Then the rose blooms, peaked in pleasure. Next, her creamy shoulders. She pulled the shift over the loose golden curls on her head and discarded the clothing on the bank.

She glowed in triumph, naked except for the black ribbon on her arm. He felt a nagging need to unwrap its mysteries, her mysteries, before his ring became hers.

The irony of her shadowy past was that, in the nude, she glowed like a sunbeam from heaven. She epitomised what he believed God had intended for man's joy. His arms ached to touch her. She waded farther out to mid-calf, and he followed. With her smile, she coaxed him in deeper until he was soaked to his thighs—shoes, pants, and the cuffs on his sleeves.

She tilted her head and a question slid from her throat. "What does God think of you now?"

Every inch of her reeked: *Take me.* Every tendon of him yearned: *Now.* Yet he understood this to be another test. God watched. Sin beckoned. The danger and anticipation heightened his desire. She wanted a challenge, so he decided to give her one.

He waded slowly closer and, touching the middle of her forehead with a fingertip, he traced the bridge of her nose, down the midline of her face, just above the skin's surface, an old skill he'd practised many times with a blade.

*Feel the blade's sharpness but do not underestimate it. Respect its dangerous potential.*

Beneath the curve of her chin, he closed his eyes and instinctively dragged his finger lower. He could detect the echo of her pulse at the hollow of her throat. Her inhales came more rapidly. At the vulnerable spot between her breasts, she held her breath, and he opened his eyes. Judging from her flush complexion, her temperature had risen several degrees.

"You think you can control your will power." She stared at his lips. "I believe you're just a man."

He shook his head *no* and combed his fingers through her hair so that several strands fell over a quivering breast. He stroked the hair over the rise and caressed the underside of the beautiful rose. The heat from his hand and her taut peak burned next to each other.

Her eyes narrowed. He liked that the tables could shift so easily in his favour.

"You're not going to say a word or give in," she half-accused. He gave her breast a slight squeeze and raised an eyebrow.

She gathered him fully into her arms. The water lapped around their legs. The ring in his pocket protruded onto her thigh, as did the thicker part of him near the entrance to Eden.

"Fere," she urged, "we don't have to wait."

Her kiss tasted like honey. Her hair, silk on his cheek. He rubbed hungrily against her body, the ring digging into his morals and her tender skin. If he relinquished control, there was no stopping them.

He dropped his hands to her hips and his mouth to her collarbone. Before she could kiss his open mouth again, he swivelled behind her and pressed into her backside. His hard groin nestled her bottom.

"Shh shh," he repeated several times through the honeyed fragrance of her hair, also in an attempt to dampen his pent-up desire. He struggled to contain his urges and stay clothed. Staying at her back was the only way he might succeed.

At first, she attempted to turn around, feigning whimpers, but he gently stroked the underside of her breasts to calm her. Murmuring her approval, she finally calmed at his touch, and he trickled lake water across her thighs and hips, hoping to dampen their passion, knowing little probably could.

He sensed it was difficult for her to let him lead. Without either of them having uttered a word, he had learned that she disliked being second in command. She fidgeted a little at his exploring caresses on her belly and breasts. She locked and un-locked her knees and tried kissing him, but his lips stayed on her shoulder, his tongue softly circling the white skin on her back. He gently tipped her chin down to signal her to watch his handiwork below and find pleasure in letting him take over.

His hand passed across her mound gently once, twice, again. The tips of his fingers ruffled her soft fur and her belly filled in anticipation of each ensuing pass. The thought of exploring her lush garden with any part of his hand excited him more. Yet he focused on her. Later, he repeatedly re-minded himself, his pleasure would come first.

He glided his fingertips to the opening between her legs. The petals had swollen and moistened. He started slow-motion runs between her legs and delved deeper into the fleshy centre, up and down the passage he wanted to enter whole as a man. He stroked forward and back and listened to her cues. At times, she held her breath, and he paused and lingered with small pulses of his fingertip. The pitch inside her built and her legs parted. Her hand covered his, follow-ing his direction, and her eyes fluttered and closed. Her chest rose, in and out, like his motions. He bit her earlobe and thrust two fingers deep where her yearning lived. And again. And again. Her fingers rode his high inside her. Their mo-tions became one. She ground her bottom into the front of his pants and their rhythm rolled into pangs of pleasure.

Buried in the back of her hair, he kissed her open-mouthed, making a soft patch of blond and skin as wet as his hand. Lake water lapped around their legs. He moaned in excesses of pleasure and physicality. He rubbed himself against her, and his fingers—their fingers—became slicker until her body constricted. The peak of desire pierced her from within. She held his hand inside her for the final rush of the climatic waterfall. Triggered by her release, his own followed the next instant. His knees nearly gave way, but he braced them both upright through the final wave.

Wild-headed in the moment, their ragged breathing synchronised and slowed. He rested his damp forehead on her backbone and hugged her, whispering a short private prayer of thanks that he had stayed clothed, a wisp away from the most egregious sin. Water rippled against their legs and soaked his pocket, where the ring laid forgotten. He took her hands in his and rinsed them in the lake. After which, he guided her hand inside his pocket, where she discovered the ring.

"What does God think of me now?" he asked over her shoulder. He lifted her hand to his mouth, kissed the ring on her finger and, full of himself, answered his own question. "God will forgive me, for I am the sovereign."

•   •   •

Anne swam in the nude while Athos stretched out on the sunny bank and watched. He worried little about whom or what came upon them. His cup runneth over.

He also experienced none of the shame that had trailed him after their previous near misses. Maybe her agreeing to be his wife made today's near-miss seem less sinful.

She swam on her back with her arms swirling like wings. She'd bob up to see if he was watching and, as soon as she had his attention, would turn over and dive, showing off her gorgeous rump. He thought her immodesty was refreshing, God's original plan for men and women in paradise.

"You look pleased with yourself," she said as she ambled in front of him, dripping water onto the tops of his bare feet. Sunlight chased every pattern of water down her drenched body. He patted the blanket next to him. He imagined many, many more afternoons to come when he could swim with her and take her whenever the urge struck.

"And why shouldn't I be?" he said and smiled.

Anne fluidly reclined on her side next to him. She rung the water from her long hair, untwisted the length, and tossed it behind her back. The water on her breasts beckoned to be lapped up, but Athos checked himself. She was as close to a real-life angel as he could imagine. He wanted God to bless their union.

"You puzzle me," she started.

"Me?" He laughed before she could go on. "I wear my family history on my sleeve, unlike someone I know." Unable to resist, he brushed off a droplet clinging to her nipple.

She readjusted the black ribbon on her arm. It stayed tightly wound despite being wet.

"Or am I wrong?" He watched intently. "You do wear something on your sleeve."

"An old memory."

"Tell me."

"It's for my parents," she said, her face sternly in control. "It was my childish way of mourning their death. Now, I can't seem to take it off."

He reached for her elbow below the ribbon but she nimbly shifted. He decided not to push the subject. "Since my father's passing last year, I haven't been able to move his shoes," he said. "They're still by his bedside."

"I don't have any tokens to remember my parents. We were paupers the summer my mother died."

"I admire your ability to survive."

"Death focuses life's purpose," she said. "But you live life ... from the balcony."

"Perhaps. But I try to stay faithful to God while also being privileged." He nodded for her agreement. She nodded back. "I could use my wealth and power for excess. But it's shallow and the main reason that I avoid Paris. Most nobles there hunt for pleasure and political favours like I would a stag. I prefer the quiet here."

"It could hurt you." Her brow knitted, and she looked across the lake. "Marrying me, for instance ..." A breeze rushed across the water's surface and disturbed the calm.

He gently turned her face back to study it. "Second thoughts?"

"Of course not," she said and lifted her chin from his grasp. "You just surprise me."

He leaned in for a kiss. "I'm not concerned about your past."

"Why not?"

"It wasn't your fault." He followed her gaze to the opposite side of the lake, where a crane stalked and snapped at the surface.

"Still—" Her small voice yielded to a short sigh. "I shouldn't have told you. I never tell anyone."

He stroked her damp hair, which was beginning to dry and curl around the frame of her face. Her past evoked unimaginable scenes—the priest in the enclave coming to her, having his way, and her living in fear of being turned out if discovered.

"Why did you tell me?" he asked.

She fell on her back and looked into the sun, squinting. "I don't know."

"I do. You trusted me." He wiped the last of the water off her breasts. "Look how comfortable we are together. I'm honoured to earn your trust."

She turned her squint onto him. "Do you trust me?"

"I have no reason not to," he said, closing in for her neck. "It's the foundation of love."

She placed a hand on his chest. "Then you love me?"

The question set him back. He hadn't yet told her *I love you*. Nor she, him. The last time he had probed his own feelings was when he'd kissed Demi, who still lingered in the back of his mind. In every other way, he burned for Anne. Yet.

*Why is Demi still inside me?*

"Do I love you?" he asked rhetorically, hoping a boyish smile would hide his confusion. "Fair question for a fiancé."

"So you do love me?" Her face froze in anticipation of his answer, and he weighed the consequences of the truth—that he just didn't know yet. He chose his words one by one.

"I'm as close to being in love with you as any woman ever before."

Emotionless, she sat up and hugged her legs against her chest. "You've had feelings like this for another woman."

Athos sat up, too, and ran his hands through his hair. He was sweating under the strong sunlight. "I ... I've been very close to *wanting* to love someone," he said in an attempt at honesty. He was also trying to push Demi from his thoughts. Demi's face. Demi's kiss.

"Who?" She squeezed her legs tighter against her chest.

He sighed. "I'm a man, Anne. I've had other women, as you've had other men."

Her expression sizzled in his direction. *Wrong answer.* He ran a hand up and down the fine down of blond hair on her arm. "I want to marry *you*."

"Under certain conditions."

He understood where she was going. "Yes, optimally, I'd like my priest to conduct the Mass. Yes, I'd also like my oldest friend to be here for the wedding. Those two conditions are reasonable."

She leapt to her feet and crossed the bank for her garment, crumpled and astray. She slipped it over her head and shook loose the clumps of her drying hair. He never recalled such beauty in an act of anger. "Anne, please, I'm ready to love. You're the woman I want." *Whom I should want.*

"Then *love me*," she demanded. "Love me as if the world will end tomorrow. Love me as if there will never be another. Love me and relinquish all others. That's the kind of love I need." She folded her arms over her breasts. The ring caught the sunlight. "That's who *I* am."

His heart melted into the sky. "Give me your hand in marriage, and I'll give you everything I have."

She sprinted toward the treeline. As soon as she disappeared, he regretted neither had possessed the courage to say *I love you.*

# Time Runs Out

Right after breakfast the next morning, Father Luc arrived on Athos's doorstep. Rather than stroll through the gardens, the priest insisted they sit across from each other at the long study table in the library.

"Two issues," Father Luc started and shot up an index finger. "The first concerns your provincial duties."

Beneath the table, Athos dug his thumbnail into the crease of a palm.

"Athos, your lack of interest in magisterial decisions is having negative consequences."

"That's my magistrate's business, not yours," Athos challenged.

"It becomes my business when the magistrate skips Mass and confession because he's short-handed and distressed about his missing son."

Athos shook his head. Bronte's absence was not his problem. "I can't control when Bronte will return to his post or when he'll send news of his whereabouts."

"Help his father. He needs your assistance and your moral support."

Athos threw up his hands. Who would advocate for his own needs? "I'm trying to remedy my most pressing problem. A wife. An heir."

"And that brings us to problem number two," Father Luc said, two fingers up.

Athos gritted his teeth. "You met with Anne without me."

"I did." Father Luc spoke so calmly that it gave Athos the opposite impression—as a lid about to blow. "Since that meeting, I've been paid another, rather unpleasant, visit by her brother."

"Father de Breuil came to see you?"

"Minutes before I was to retire last night, he arrived outside my private quarters and insisted that we speak. I was in my night clothes." Father Luc looked down at himself and shuddered. "Father de Breuil insinuated himself inside. He's as assertive in person as you say he is in the pulpit."

Athos's stomach churned. A confrontation between curates was just what he didn't need. But why, after Anne had received his ring, would Father de Breuil be out on a night rampage?

Father Luc sighed. "He saw you two together at Agape Lake."

Locking stares in silence, Father Luc's stern nod punched Athos between the eyes. Athos crumpled under the weight of the disappointment. He dropped his head into his hands and dug his elbows into the wood table.

"You didn't heed my advice, Athos."

*Useless, useless advice.* Anne represented a choice between paradise and sin, and in her presence the path of good intentions shifted like mercury in a maze. Athos couldn't deny anything but the hard facts. "She also departed in a huff," he admitted, aware he was throwing fuel onto his funeral pyre.

"Father de Breuil is livid about the whole incident. He's due here any minute to strike the sword of God on your conscience."

Athos swallowed and looked up. "How much did he see?"

"I'll spare you his version of events."

Athos's head fell back, and he groaned in dread. It wasn't that he didn't deserve to be put in his place, but there was also a high likelihood the priest would bar Athos from seeing Anne.

"I advised Father de Breuil to send Anne away, far away," Father Luc said in a much quieter voice.

Athos gripped the edge of the table. "You're supposed to be *my* advocate."

"I am your advocate." Father Luc pointed down toward Hell. "You're listening to the devil in your loins. Or I could also say, the devil who dances in your eyes."

Athos pushed away from the table and knocked over the chair at the writing desk behind him. "Why in God's name would her brother watch us?"

"He's her guardian. He has a right."

"And I'm the sovereign. I have the right!"

Father Luc turned his face away from Athos and rubbed the bridge of his nose. "Unfortunately for your soul, that's true. However, I believe you want to live rightly by God."

Athos wanted to laugh and cry at the same time. The struggle between his morals and his manhood tensed every nerve. As he was about to rant in frustration, the library door opened with a thud. Father de Breuil stood in the opening, his face as red as the Cardinal's robes.

Arrogantly, Athos flung out his arms and made an exaggerated bow. If he were to be labelled a libertine, he might as well enjoy the ride to infamy.

Father de Breuil's face puckered in disapproval. "Monsieur de la Fere—"

"Comte," Athos corrected. "I am *Comte* de la Fere."

Father Luc softly grunted in the background but Athos ignored the warning. What else did he have to lose in his topsy-turvy life?

"Welcome to Valliere, Father de Breuil." Athos righted the toppled chair, placed it at the head of the long table and motioned for the priest to sit. The priest stared first at Athos then Father Luc before marching toward the seat.

"You know why I am here, I take it?" Father de Breuil asked as he squared his back against the seat.

"Of course," Athos said and resumed his place on the bench, "you have come to reconcile the virtue of your sister. Shall we get down to business?"

Both priests stared slightly askance at Athos, as if he had just spouted nonsense.

"I want to marry your sister. I've told her my intentions and she's agreed—" Father de Breuil opened his mouth to speak, but Athos spoke louder, "—and I have given her my mother's ring. There's only one more step before we can wed, which is to receive the church's blessing."

"Monsieur," Father de Breuil, nostrils flared, finally inserted himself into the conversation, "excuse me, *Comte*. You've taken liberties with my charge that require me to speak up. You've engaged in sinful acts. You perpetuated those acts in blatant disregard of her virtue. In broad daylight. You tempted her with wickedness of the flesh, a kind which I've never been exposed to!"

"And because you were exposed," Athos said, disgusted by the priest's hypocrisy, "you can also testify to it. You could, for instance, swear before God which of us at the lake was bathing nude."

The accuser shook his head. "You have no right—"

"I have every right! It falls within my duties to decide who has been wronged and mete out a judgment. So, I'll ask again. Who at the lake was unclothed?"

Father Luc reached out to touch Athos's hand, but he slid it under the table. For now, Athos liked taking charge. "Father de Breuil, will you or will you not bless this marriage? It's a simple question that requires either a yes or a no."

"It's not a simple question," Father Luc butted in. "And as your priest, I advocate against it, as does Father de Breuil."

"Against it?" the second priest questioned, his eyebrows high on his forehead. "I'm not against it. Quite the contrary. I believe he *must* marry my sister immediately before they wander farther down the path of sin. If Anne becomes ill-reputed, all hope for her future is lost. You must marry her!"

Athos straightened his back and let the words sink in. *Must marry her.* The irony was almost too much.

"The alternative is unacceptable," Father de Breuil reasserted. "Father Luc, surely you see this is the only way."

"No, I do not!"

Athos tried reaching for his priest's hand, this time, the one to be denied. "I want to marry her," Athos told Father Luc, "and now I can."

"You don't know what you want!" Father Luc jolted from the bench, fists tight. "She should be sent to a convent. If what I've heard about her is true, her conduct is reprehensible. Even when she is fully clothed. How else could you explain your fall, Athos? She's fallen, and you'll fall with her."

"My sister's moral conduct is mine to judge and safeguard!" Father de Breuil shouted.

"Then wake up," Father Luc shot back. "You can't even admit it when you've *been exposed*."

Athos met Father Luc on the other side of the table. "Father, I want your blessing. This union could solve many problems."

"Not in my opinion. It will only bring more." Father Luc sidestepped Athos and headed for the door. He hesitated before passing Father de Breuil and dropped a parting message. "Blood often blinds us from the truth."

The slam of the door echoed in the room for several moments. In the subsequent long silence, Athos moved to his writing desk and took out a quill and paper.

"What are you doing?" Father de Breuil sighed over Athos's shoulder.

"Asking a friend for a favour."

# Teardrops and Fire

The letter worked. Demi arrived at the front of Father Luc's church the minute mid-week evensong had ended. Athos kept lookout from a hideaway across the street. Without anyone else the wiser, Athos settled in to watch Demi convince Father Luc to bless Anne as his wife.

It had taken tremendous audacity to ask her for help. His letter pleading for Demi's assistance had been the most difficult he'd ever written. He had attempted to come across as both humble and logical. Humble, to apologise for kissing her and soiling her loyalty to Bronte. Logical, because Athos and Demi needed to break the bond of their attraction. In reward for her help, Athos had dangled an incentive – he would use leverage to put an end to Bronte's arranged marriage. He would bestow a title without compensation in exchange for his family's blessing. Bronte would earn a title. True love would prevail. Everyone would win.

Athos chose a lookout from above, on the low-pitched tile roof of the *Deux Colombes*, where the innkeeper was glad to grant access in exchange for a break on taxes. He knelt behind a short wooden box for dry storage. After the evening service let out, the crowd mingled around the stone steps near the entrance. Demi had skipped evensong and had approached the church from the square. As soon as Athos spotted her, he took quick glances from his hiding place. Laughter and loud children made the scene below light-hearted, but Athos was anything but. In a grey dress and short jacket trimmed in black, Demi looked as keyed up as he felt inside.

Without delay, she made her way to Father Luc, who was filling his lungs with the early evening's cool air. Reaching him, Demi curtsied and the priest greeted her with a broad smile of welcome. She launched into a long talk, and the longer she spoke, the flatter Father Luc's smile became. Athos craned to read her lips, make out any words or phrases he could, but he was too far away. Demi hesitated several times and darted her eyes to catch any eavesdroppers. The crowd thinned out, and she continued to speak, and at one point, she clutched the priest's forearm. He clasped her wrist and drew her nearer. Father Luc listened, frowned once or twice, and after a few more long sentences from Demi, he did something that bewildered Athos altogether.

He appeared to dry a tear from her cheek.

Scuffing his boots, Athos crawled madly on his stomach for a better view from the ledge, but Father Luc swiftly escorted

Demi inside the church, a comforting arm around her shoulder. Athos jumped to his feet and wiped the back of a hand across his gaping mouth. *What have I just seen? Why would she cry?* Damned to wait it out, he slumped on the edge of the storage box and wracked his brain for an appropriate saint to lift a prayer.

God granted him no reprieve. Instead, the twist of his machinations tightened. Unexpectedly, Anne appeared at the church steps below. She oozed her trademark smugness and began to take each step like a lioness. Athos shot straight up, too stunned to care about hiding. He marvelled at her commanding presence. Her hair draped in ringlets from underneath a feathered hat. A yellow chiffon dress flowed behind her. A few men in the low evening light interrupted their conversations to stare at her. She smiled back. For a split-second, he was both jealous and proud.

Then he remembered Demi. Anne couldn't meet her. Not now.

Anne was three or four strides away from the door. If he called out, what would he say in defence of his whereabouts? That he had been bird-watching? Studying cloud formations? Maybe she just required a break from the late afternoon heat. Or, more likely, she was taking matters into her own hands with Father Luc. She'd already approached him once without his knowledge.

"Anne!" he shouted just as the door to the church sealed her inside. He bolted for the roof's hatch.

Down into the larder, Athos took the ladder three rungs at a time and surged toward the front door, frightening the innkeeper. He landed on the street in a damp sweat. No one was left in the area in front of the church. Its tall doors of solid hardwood stretched up like sentinels, demanding a good explanation for his passage. He couldn't think of a single one and didn't know whether bursting inside would do his case any good.

*What have I done?*

Demi. Anne.

Teardrops. Fire.

He found a shaded nook under an arch and laid his forehead on the cut stone. Time crept by as he kept watch on the doors. It could have been ten minutes or twenty. It was long enough for him to reconsider his faulty plan. But the doors opened and Demi emerged. Rushing to her side, she startled when he grabbed her by the arm.

Her eyes told him she'd cried more than one tear. She shook her head and leaned away from his hold. "Athos," she said, "please let me pass. I must go as soon as possible. I have news of Bronte."

He tightened his grip, more in shock than to stop her. "Bronte sent you a message?"

Demi pulled to no avail. "Let me go, and I'll tell you what I know."

Though he reeled for information about her conversation with Father Luc—and now Bronte—Athos shook himself from dismay. "Of course, of course," he said and released her.

Demi smoothed her sleeve and took a step back. He remembered how full she made his heart, and he suffered to think he may have hurt her.

"Bronte's been seen in Paris," she said. "I must find a messenger at once to send a letter."

"How do you know?"

"Anne." Demi glanced back at the church doors. "She sent word to her friends at Court and told them to notify her if he surfaced in Paris. She's found him. He's staying at the salon in the *Hôtel de Rambouillet*."

"How long?"

"About a week. She says she heard of it today. She showed us the note from her contact."

Athos surrendered his wits and stumbled a few steps backwards. Had he been better at his only role, as the head of an entire province, it would have been *his* contacts who had found Bronte. As it were, his connections were few and far afield.

"Don't blame yourself," Demi said, though she didn't reach for him. Instead, she glanced again at the church doors, and Athos recognised something in her he'd never seen.

"You're frightened," he said. "What happened in there?"

Dazed, Demi slowly gathered her skirt to leave. "It's worse than I had imagined."

"What's worse? Did you speak with Father Luc? Is all hope lost for my cause?"

The light left her eyes. "The last time we met, I asked you if you loved her. Do you know now? Are you in love with Anne?"

Athos desired to pull Demi into his arms and find the real answer. Know who to love. Know who to trust. Know where his heart lived.

"It's as I said in my letter," he pleaded. "This is the right course for me. *She* is the right course." He shook his head in hopes it would shake Demi from the wrong direction. "How could it—we—be any different?"

"I couldn't lie to Father Luc," she murmured and looked down her skirt. "I told him you were having doubts."

"You told him about us?" The words caught in his throat.

"No. But I didn't advocate for your marriage." She looked up, the spark of hope gone. "I said I thought you were in love with someone else."

Athos nearly fell to his knees. He understood her tears. In the oncoming twilight, he held her sweet words close, for her body was forbidden. "Demi," he spoke softly and closed in so he could look directly into her face. "She has my ring."

"She has more than your ring," she said and pivoted from his gaze. "I must go."

"Wait." He caught her by the shoulders and situated her before him. "What do you mean it's worse than you imagined?"

She shook her head and closed her eyes. "She's … she's …"

The church bell tolled and in the sudden vibration, Demi dodged his tender hold on her. A little of his heart careened down the street after her.

When the chimes ceased, he spun back to the church front. Anne anchored one door open as wide as it would go.

"Did she tell you Bronte's in Paris?"

He nodded and shifted his weight. *What had she seen? Did it make any difference?* All arrows pointed in her direction.

"Let me guess," he said, kicking up dust as he moved forward. "You're here to make a stand."

One side of her mouth turned up. "I reminded Father Luc that you're the sovereign. Your rule supersedes the church's. He didn't like being reminded."

At the bottom step, he lifted his arms toward her. The pieces of the puzzle might never be perfect, only her beauty earned that rank.

"I also came to see you," she said and floated down a few steps, "about Bronte."

He dropped his arms to his side and frowned. The subject raised the hair on his neck.

"I wanted to find Bronte to give him a chance to be here for our wedding," she said.

"I'm thankful you've found him and a little miffed I didn't. But now that we can reach him, we must."

"And what will you do if he doesn't come home?" she asked. "Will you marry me?"

Athos chuckled a little under his breath. Marrying her would close the door on his doubt, if his confusion about Demi was just doubt. Though seconds ago, Demi's eyes had elicited something deeper in him. Part of him wanted to retrace his steps in the last few weeks. Part of him felt he might never see Demi again. Beneath Anne's gaze, the thought needled his conscience, stung him like a bee. He pulled Anne down the last few treads and into his arms.

"Bronte will come," he said and nuzzled her hair, a sweet field of honeysuckle on her neck.

She drew his lips to hers. "He has seven days before Gregori sends me away."

# And God Created All

Seven days. A week. Though it smacked of biblical heavy-handedness, Athos wasn't fazed by Father de Breuil's deadline for a wedding. Changing course now seemed absurd. Athos wanted to marry Anne, had made every attempt to win her, and had asked his church in good faith for a blessing. That the consent to marry had come from a priest who happened to be his bride's guardian might have complicated matters for a man of lesser status. For a sovereign, any course could be justified. Even the end of a marriage.

Nonetheless, Athos resolved to talk to Father Luc one last time. He waited a few days to put distance between Demi's visit and his own. On Saturday morning, Athos tracked his priest down in the church flower garden, where he was pruning roses.

Seeing Athos, a gloveless Father Luc seized a stem too quickly and drew blood on the pad of his thumb, which he stuck in his mouth. Before he spoke, Father Luc pulled it out, squinted at it and tightened his fingers around the sore.

"I didn't expect to see you this soon," he said.

"I had to try one more time."

"Try? You weren't trying when you sent Demi. You were hiding. Great men don't hide nor do they send fragile women to do their bidding." Father Luc shoved his fist into the robe that covered his wide belly.

"She's my only advocate. Or, I thought she was."

"She's honest and hurt. What I don't understand is how you could turn your back on the feelings you have for her."

"She didn't tell you that."

"She didn't need to." Father Luc shook his head. "Athos, I've seen and done many things in my life. These complications are very ordinary. How a man deals with obstacles is what makes him who he is. But I have the feeling you're not here to right any wrongs."

Athos bit his tongue and wondered if anything would change the priest's mind. "I'm marrying Anne this Wednesday. Her brother will perform the ceremony in Averdon."

Father Luc's jaw muscles flexed. "You won't wait for Bronte?"

"We've sent our swiftest courier to Paris. Bronte will have a day to spare."

"Why not longer? Are you in such a hurry you can't wait? What are you thinking in that head of yours?"

Athos filled his chest. He wished the priest was less intent on this interrogation. The jolly old soldier-turned-curate seemed to have vanished since their first swim at Agape Lake.

"Bronte introduced us. He encouraged this match. Waiting will only end in Anne being sent to a convent."

"It'll give you perspective. Anne is the kind of woman who can consume you."

"Her intensity appeals to me."

"And spurs you to rash decisions." Father Luc sighed. "Wait for Bronte. That's all I ask."

"So I lose her? And harbour more doubt?"

"You admit you have it."

Athos pivoted and tromped through a row of azaleas. He never liked the bushes because they only bloomed once a year.

Father Luc followed him and offered him the sheers. "Think of a few extra days as time to pull out the insidious weeds from your thoughts."

Athos grabbed the tool and shoved the blades into the ground between bushes. "I don't weed."

"You'll never disavow that streak of aristocratic privilege in your blood, will you? Kings usually suffer the worst."

"I'm not a king, and up until now, I've rarely used my position for anything other than making decisions for my people and the land. There's nothing wrong with me indulging it now."

"Oh, but you see," Father Luc said and raised a finger, "there's everything wrong with it if it blinds you to the truth."

A slap on the face might have felt better. Athos sneered and yanked the sheers from the ground. He headed for the roses, which were bright with red blooms. One rough snip after another, he chopped a dozen stems to the ground. Then he dropped the sheers and gripped the roses in a bundle, suffering from several thorn pricks of his own. As he bled, he stood waiting for a sign, sceptical that omens arrived when they were most needed.

Father Luc stuck out his thumb, where a small scab had formed. "Small cuts heal. As for the mistakes you're about to make in your life, I'm less confident."

The priest picked up the sheers and left the garden. Athos clutched the bouquet and bled alone a while longer.

•   •   •

Athos had agreed for Anne to visit his château at Valliere one more time before the wedding, the same day as his failed appeal to Father Luc.

Athos had no good news to share with Anne after Father Luc abandoned him in the garden, and he didn't feel like talking.

At home, Athos's preparations for the wedding were in motion, except that his plans ran against tradition. He wasn't hosting a village-wide celebration or inviting dignitaries from other provinces to attend. He planned the exact opposite. He had informed his entire staff no one was to be in the vicinity of his estate for the entire month after the wedding. He desired privacy with his new wife.

"Why so gloomy?" Anne asked Athos at the front door. He took her arm and led her through the garden, a blanket in tow. Dusk was still an hour away.

"Why do you think?"

Anne laughed, the kind of laugh a woman uses to hide an inside joke. "I know something that would make you take your mind off of Father Luc."

He gently removed her wandering hand from his bottom and refocused her on the walking path. "We need to wait a little longer."

"I didn't mean *that*," she said and pulled a small book from her wrist satchel. "I've brought my copy of Shakespeare."

He smiled weakly and directed them toward a small hill that buffered the garden from the pond. He laid the blanket on the grass and reclined flat on his back. She followed suit, but lay on her stomach and propped the book on his diaphragm. The book rose and fell when he inhaled and exhaled.

"You're a beautiful man," she said up on her elbows, flipping through pages.

He smiled across his body at her. "It sounds odd to describe a man as beautiful. You, on the other hand ..."

He brushed her hair down her back once and put his hands behind his head—the safest place for them.

"How shall you love me?" she asked.

"I'm not sure I understand your question." He gazed into a cloud passing overhead.

"How—as in what *way*."

"Is this what women discuss before their wedding day?"

"Open your heart wide, Fere, if you want me inside it."

The cloud curled into a swirl. "I think a boundless love is possible between us."

"Tell me how I make you feel."

The flame in her eyes lit a small fire within him. "You're provoking me to seduce you," he said.

"You haven't so far."

His quick huff caused the book to tumble to his side opposite from her. "I haven't won you over yet?"

"I said you haven't seduced me," she exclaimed.

Athos sat up. She rolled on her back, and her head came to rest at the crook of his leg and groin. The devilish smile on her face taunted him as did any slight motion of her head.

"What happened between us at Agape Lake then?" he asked. "It riled every priest within a crow's flight of here."

"You teased me. Much different than seduction."

"And my poems to you? Those weren't seductive?"

"Close. But they were merely your simpering heart on paper."

"And who's teasing whom now?" He wanted to kiss her and fondle a bosom, but thought better. "Let me see that book."

He grabbed it from the grass, and she nestled her head deeper into his hip.

He flipped hastily through a few pages. "I shall read if you promise to stop moving your head."

She giggled but became still.

"Here," he said, not certain whether he was interested in tamping down her sexual spirit again or rousing it. "*How can it? O, how can Love's eye be true / That is so vex'd with watching and with tears? / No marvel then, though I mistake my view / The sun itself sees not till heaven clears.*"

She grabbed the book from his hands and laid it over her heart. "Come down here. Into me."

He closed in on her parted lips. Her eyes shut as she finished the verse. "*O cunning Love! with tears thou keep'st me blind / Lest eyes well-seeing thy foul faults should find.*"

"You keep me blind," he whispered above her mouth. "I'm not the seducer, but the seduced."

No kiss followed. More poems did. She knew every son-net by memory. Every one. He realised this after the fifth and the sixth, after he stopped checking passages against her recitations. The poetry gave him a safe passage to think about her body in a manner he couldn't act on until the wed-ding. He could justify caressing her wrist or stroking her cheek, but under the spell of her voice, he indulged many more fantasies of their ultimate union. Her eyes told him she was doing the same.

On the grassy hill, he basked in her sun, guiltlessly thank-ful that pleasure—not virtue—would come first in a few days time.

# His Final Confession

Athos's last quandary was deciding who would hear his pre-marital confession. He needed to absolve himself of Demi. Neither priest was the ideal keeper of this unfortunate information.

Even though Father Luc suspected, a full confession about what had happened with Demi would solidify his disapproval of Athos's marriage to Anne. In the hands of Father de Breuil, Athos's faithfulness to Anne would come into question. In the end, the night before the ceremony, Athos sought out Father de Breuil. He trusted the man would guard the confession with his saintly life.

As he entered the confessional at the church in Averdon, a blasphemous memory surfaced, that of Anne in the same place many weeks ago, pleasuring herself on the day that Athos had come to meet her brother. The smile on his face faded when the adjacent door slapped shut.

After a short call-and-response in Latin, Athos began. He pecked at the words, rather than ploughed.

"Forgive me, Father, for I have sinned. It's been several weeks since my last confession. I believe you know why."

"I believe you're here to appease me rather than God."

The Adam's apple in his throat stuck in place. He'd hoped for a smoother start.

"I chose you because—"

"—because I'm a sympathetic ear?"

"Because you see the merit in my choice to marry Anne. But there's more I need to say. It goes deeper than this marriage."

Father de Breuil coughed softly. "Go on."

"I need your understanding. Everything in my life seems to have changed in a short time. Since my father's death, I've lost everyone – my priest, my friend Bronte. All these losses have made me wallow in self-pity."

"Quite natural," came the reaction between the slated-wood partition.

"And," Athos paused, "unfortunately, I've behaved inappropriately with Anne. I ask for God's forgiveness and for yours, as well. Please forgive me, Father. A man's urges can cripple his conviction, and in Anne's case, they've nearly crushed mine."

The priest issued a brief prayer.

"I've also committed other sins—" Athos waited several seconds. "—sins involving another woman."

A dense silence filled the compartments.

"Father de Breuil?"

"Who's the other sinner?" the priest blurted.

"It wasn't our intention nor do I understand why it happened."

The priest over-emphasised each word. "*With whom?*"

"A lifelong friend. It didn't go beyond a few kisses—"

"A few?"

"Two. Only two."

"But what sordid path did your thoughts take you?"

Athos rubbed his eyes. "Places I wish they hadn't."

The priest's next response carried an uncharacteristic sarcasm. "Yet you marry my sister tomorrow. You cannot have two women in your heart and head. It creates Hell."

Athos grabbed a fistful of his own hair. "Absolve me then."

"I'm stunned. All the self-control you've exercised with my sister now seems disingenuous."

*Control?* "But I thought you were outraged by my behaviour?"

Father de Breuil raised his voice. "Anne needs singular devotion. She's a woman of great demands and great needs."

"Which I intend to fulfil."

The priest continued, almost in afterthought. "And more importantly, so does God."

"I love Anne." Athos had no idea that he would say it or any comprehension why he was saying it now.

"Have you told her?"

"No."

A heavy sigh came from the priest's compartment. "God sees into your heart, Comte."

*Always. Always.* "I wish to be cleansed. I wish to go to Anne whole."

"Then pray for mercy."

"Will you also forgive me?"

"Forgiveness will be harder won from your new wife."

"You must not tell her, *cannot* tell her," Athos said, his mouth pressed against the barrier.

"Of course not," Father de Breuil said smoothly. "Your own heart will betray you if you don't devote every particle of your being to her."

The priest uttered a closing prayer, a penance, and an absolution before he opened and closed his door.

Left behind in a thick incense, Athos struggled to speak. "May it be so."

Part

# III

# THE GARDEN OF EDEN

*And the serpent said unto the woman,*
*Ye shall not surely die: for God knows that when*
*you eat of it your eyes will be opened,*
*and you will be like God, knowing good and evil.*
*– Book of Genesis*

# Athos's Log, Midnight

*My bedroom is dark, save for one candle. The house is emptied of sounds and demands and servants. Tomorrow, Anne will be with me at Valliere in my most private sanctuary. I need to end my isolation and loneliness. I regret Bronte is only a distant concern and not by my side. My father's Bible weighs heavily in my lap. In these moments before first light of my new life, I wonder about Adam and Eve, once the only beings on Earth. The beginners of procreation. They began love. They began lust. They bestowed meaning to woman with man.*

# First Light

At noon, Athos stood at the altar of the church in Averdon. Anne, in gold-threaded cream silk, stood beside him. Her brother performed the ceremony flawlessly. The priest's short sermon left no lasting impression on Athos. He was too enrapt by his new possession.

Porcelain skin. Blue eyes. Golden hair. Everything else was a superfluous backdrop.

Athos gave pause only at the end. During the final prayer, which sealed the two as one, the priest delivered the lines with an unbroken gaze on Anne. On the way out of the church, her brother lightly kept a hand on the small of her back. He didn't break contact until she crossed the threshold to the other side.

Inside the homebound carriage, Athos wrestled for words. "You're so quiet," she started.

"Awestruck," he said softly, "over you."

"My brother says you have something to tell me."

He nodded and finally spoke it. "I love you."

Her eyes began to smile before her mouth.

He took her hands, removed her gloves and brought her warm hands to his cheek. "And you?"

"I love you, Fere."

He waited to kiss her until they stepped out of the carriage in front of Valliere. Athos gave the coachman final instructions and sent him away. Alone at last, he took one long look at her, the inexplicable mistress of his new life.

In the foyer, he led her to an adjacent, small music room, adorned in deep reds and dark wood walls. A pianoforte, a harp, and several plush chairs covered in dark red upholstery ringed the room. In the middle, he'd placed a small canopied bed, barely wide enough for two. The down comforter had been turned down.

She glided to the end of the canopy and began a short soliloquy about where she had imagined they would first make love, perhaps under a tent in the field, at the bank of the pond, in his father's large bed somewhere upstairs, on the chaise in the library. Athos shook his head and smiled wider with each guess.

"Or your room," she said.

"You'll have to earn that privilege," he teased, which caused her to pout as playfully.

"I'm your wife. I shouldn't have to."

"Share all of yourself with me," he said more seriously, glancing at the black ribbon on her arm, "all the mysteries, and you'll earn the right to mine."

His comeback rolled off her shoulders.

"The music room?" she said, curious of the pianoforte. "Do you play?"

"I will tonight."

He lit two candelabras and the red hues in the room sharpened. This château—his private refuge for so long—now protected another. Yet within its walls, he wanted her to surrender, not just to desire, but to love.

"Will you be vulnerable to me this first night, Anne?" He circled around the room and watched her body cues carefully. He loosened his collar and unbuttoned his cuffs.

"Anything you wish." She undid a button on her creamy bodice.

"Don't," he said softly, waving her hands down. He searched for the right words. He needed her to know she didn't have to be the seductress.

She squirmed subtly and dropped her arms.

Moving in front of her, he lifted her face to his and unpinned her hair. It spilled down easily and filled his lungs with her honeysuckle scent. He ventured in with small kisses atop her eyelids and high cheeks.

"You have the right to say no," he said between kisses.

"What?" she asked, pulling away.

"I won't force you to do anything you don't also desire."

She grabbed his neck and blinked in disbelief. Her blue eyes shone like sharp crystals in the crimson light.

"Trust me," he said and rubbed the backs of her hands around his neck. "I'm asking you to trust me."

He soared in the fullness of her presence. Up next to her in the quiet that he had meticulously arranged, their breathing sounded like an oncoming storm. The tempest had been building at each prior exchange between them. Every word and touch before now had been Act One.

"Anne, I want you to be with me in mutual love. Feel a sense of freedom in my devotion. You don't have to tempt me. I'm yours now."

She opened her mouth but didn't speak. Her hands fell from his neck.

He nodded. "You have my word I'll honour you."

She shivered. "No one's ever said this to me before."

He gathered up her hands and risked hurting her with his bluntness. "You've survived the only way you've known how—by using your body."

She kept still, casting her sight at a place beyond him.

"You've suffered," he went on. "I don't want to cause you any more suffering."

He placed light kisses on each cheek. "Love me in a different way. Let go of the past."

"How?" She gulped more than asked.

"Place your heart in my hands. Find shelter in me."

Her open-mouth kiss signaled the shift he'd been searching for. *Total release.* She unlocked the sensual trust he had desired from her at every previous turn.

Unwrapping her was inch-by-inch bliss. Upon every glorious feature he laid equally beautiful words and caresses. Her shoulder, a downy peach. Her nipples, brilliant starbursts. Her mound, sacred paradise. The silk of her dress seemed course compared to the down of her skin. Kneeling, he ran his hands and lips over her thighs, arousing himself to the brink, but he held back and finally laid her languid, naked body across the bed.

"Pleasure yourself first," he whispered across her lips. "If you'll allow, I'd like to watch."

Her eyes grew wide, but her lips formed *yes*. She knew how. He'd known as much. Slowly undressing himself, he watched her hands roam her body, a journey from the pout of her moist mouth to the pocket of desirous flesh beneath her belly. Each pass of her hand on her skin sent ripples over every pore of his own. All the while, she kept her eyes on him, playing him as much as she played with herself. Her fluid motions increased in fervour. With every fondle of her breasts and thrust of her fingers between her legs, she moaned his name.

"Fere," she pleaded, stretching out to touch him, "join me."

He grabbed himself before she could. "Finish, and I shall."

Her hands rediscovered her mound. She touched herself with the experience of a master, circling atop her most gratifying spot and then plunging below in the next breath. The pitch of her body, hips tipped up and then down, the motions of lovers in need, stunningly reframed his idea of the meaning of physical pleasure. He'd never watched a woman so expertly love herself. And the knowledge invigorated his deepest desire for greater heights. She beckoned him to touch himself in sync with her, and within seconds of his submission, she arched to completion. A mere witness to her sound and shudder, he drank in the image, yet resisted his own climax by a thin thread.

"How?" she asked breathlessly. "How could you hold back?"

Standing at the bedside, he bent over and kissed her belly, which quivered with latent joy.

"Knowing I'd be next."

His need to touch her body had never been greater. The heatwaves of his need swirled around the room and caused the candles to flicker. Sliding in next to her on the bed, he petted her already sensitised skin to rekindle her pleasure. Now, he didn't keep her from touching between his legs.

His body craved her possession. He could think of no poetry to recite that could take them any higher than their skin sinking into each other's. He rolled on top of her and buried one potent thrust, a collision of time and tension.

Finding a strong current of rhythm, her honey bathed his body. They tumbled over, fused together, and her hair fanned his chest. The weight and sight of her on top of him stirred what he recognised must be love, a delectable feast, an unbreakable spell. Arch after arch into her voluptuous darkness, the world parted, an experience they had denied too long.

Rocking toward surrender, she captured him, completed him, encouraged him with every upward draw and warm touch of his hands on her breasts and hips. He climbed higher in their light—the first light—of Earth and Heaven. Toward Eden, he pushed as long as his flesh could withstand until their stars united.

• • •

In the night, their lovemaking surged on like a rain-swollen river. Their exploration was boundless, a consecration of flesh and moral abandonment. The tapers in the music room burned to nubs. On the brink of sunrise, thinking they could take of each other no more, napping rekindled their arousal. The sunlight poured through the windows and exposed Anne's full glory. Her body convinced him perfection was possible. Only the black tag on her arm offset the ideal.

"Come," he said, drunk from her. "Listen."

He sat at the pianoforte, and she draped her naked body across his back and wrapped her arms loosely around his chest.

He played a few bars of a nocturne, the one he had learned from her. He turned his face so she could see his mischievous grin.

"Such an incredible melody you hummed that day in the confessional," he teased.

"You scoundrel!" she hissed in his ear. "Eavesdropping!"

Before her anger simmered more, he grabbed her around the waist and positioned her to stand facing him, between his legs and the piano. He tasted the fold beneath each breast and kissed the soft down above her belly button.

"Before now, that memory of you kept me very satisfied," he said, his hot breath against the delicate blond line of fine hair above her mound. "And hungry."

He guided her to lean slightly back against the instrument. Her bottom nudged a few discordant notes on the keys. She braced herself on the music shelf, arms apart at her sides.

He laid an ear on her lower belly, and played high and low octaves of the nocturne on the keyboard beside her hips, listening to the notes vibrate from her core. The vibrations pooled in her soft centre. Her bottom relaxed on the keys and the discordant notes rumbled low into him.

He brushed his hands down her cleavage and followed her curves to the crook of her knees, until gently he lifted each foot to rest on the bench on either side of him. Her most tender spot, an open fire throughout the night, spread before him on the keys. Its melody beckoned him to play.

He delved into her pink flesh, his tongue the maestro. He hummed the nocturne and caused her to gasp. She grasped his shoulders for support. The piano pitched, the keys randomly struck, their atonal quality also striking notes of transgression within him.

Standing, he filled her and played her to another height, as the keys banged and their rhythm intensified. Haphazard notes surrounded them. Discordant chord upon discordant chord. Wanting more, he lifted her off the piano, a reprieve, but the tune unfolded in near perfection. His strength kept them upright in tight thrusts. The bench toppled over behind him, and a shared chorus rose up between them, a note of sustained ecstasy.

•   •   •

All propriety fell away. Athos began experiencing time in cycles unrelated to light and dark but from one sensual height to the next. The nights and days ran into one. Outside of the constraints of time, they climbed and conquered desire, fell into repose, then ate or slept, and began again. He thanked God his youthful stamina had returned after his long trial of celibacy.

There were intermittent stretches of calm. She would sleep and he took to writing her poems. He often drank wine at those moments because sleep was more elusive than ever. Lost in time, his thoughts swirled around their lust. When he stepped into public again, would everyone see he'd changed? Had he?

"What are you thinking?" Her eyes were half open. Laid out on the chaise in the library, she wore one of his dressing gowns, which he'd lent her for warmth.

"That you are the sun," he said and finished a line of verse in his nearly full journal. "If I gaze too long, I won't be able to see."

"Then it's time," she said and stretched, the front of the gown opening to expose the shadow of a delicate breast.

"For what?"

"For me to see your room."

# Athos's Log, Pre-Dawn

*I am with her. In light and dark. At sunrise and midnight. I am with her.*

*My head, my hands, the blood of my body wraps around her. Time has either stopped or gone on without us. I render my heart free of its flameless past. I am inside her ~ she, inside me. The turn of the tempest has come and swept me up into a lust more powerful than logic. She holds my heart in her palms and if it beats again, it's only because she makes it.*

# 22

# Sacred Ground

"This door doesn't befit your stature as the sovereign of Berry," Anne said abruptly at his bedroom door.

Athos rested a hand on the centre panel of the narrow entrance. Compared to the other doors they'd passed in the château, his door seemed diminutive.

"But what's behind this door does befit *me*," Athos said and swung open the dark wooden portal into his interior life.

The last rays of daylight filtered in from abutting corner windows, separated by a thin strip of mullion. His room, situated in the southwest corner of the château, drew the best light, even in the oncoming dusk. Athos's mood improved each time he entered this sacred space. Vast knowledge lived inside his chamber, the secrets of minds greater than his. He felt particularly protective of it, even with Anne, because he believed no one would understand his motivation.

Up and down every wall, some in neat stacks, others in tossed-off piles and many more crammed into several book-cases, Athos kept his most cherished volumes. Books by Plato and Socrates and work by Thomas Aquinas and old copies of *Utopia*. His collection rivalled that of the downstairs library. Most Frenchmen's obsessions with social favour, or religious fervour, or political power were a shadow compared to his. Athos's obsession, prior to Anne, had been knowledge.

She spun clockwise, then counter-clockwise, absorbing the monumental storehouse of words.

"How in the world did you find all of these?" Her aura glowed, a relief to Athos. Unlike Bronte, who'd scoffed at his collections, Anne appreciated the effort.

"An unparalleled network of booksellers. I've found them in every port from here to the Orient," he said, slipping on a pair of pants laid out over his tucked bed.

She pouted for him not to get dressed on her account. He brought her a thin book from his nightstand.

"This book," he said, which he admired front and back before handing over, "comes from Turkey."

"Do you know Turkish?" She rubbed the brown leather cover and sniffed the spine. "It even smells exotic."

"It's their interpretation of how their god Muhammad ascends toward Heaven with the help of the archangel Gabriel." He rubbed her back, warm beneath his night shirt, which she wore more regally than a royal cape. "I can only read the title, *The Progress of the Prophet*."

"Why own it if you cannot read it?" She hugged the book to her chest.

He smoothed a strand of her hair and tilted his face into hers. "I believe you know," he whispered, "that possession is half of fulfilment."

She kissed the cover of the book then him. "May I keep it for a while?" she asked.

He opened his arms to the room. "They're all yours now." His offer satisfied him to a degree he hadn't felt since the last time he lent a book to ... to Demi.

He backed into a post of his canopied bed, remembering she still had several of his volumes on gardening.

"You need rest," Anne said. She forced him to sit on the edge of bed. She lay her cheek on his forehead. "You're pale, probably from exertion."

He nodded and stretched out, keen to any sign that Anne recognised his guilt. Demi pained his conscience.

"Ah," Anne said, reaching across him to the next pillow. "Perhaps I'm not the only source of your exertion."

The Chinese pillow book lay open to a double-page spread. Anne's grin turned into a throaty laugh. He tried to catch her wrist before she took hold of the erotic manual, but she gathered it up deliciously and sprawled over his torso to get a better look. "I believe we've tried this."

The page showed a couple reclining on their sides, the man entering the woman from behind while his hand touched the button of flesh between her legs. Bold red ink coloured every pleasure point on the woman—nipples, mouth, and the tip of her mound.

"If I didn't think you were exhausted," she said and tapped the picture, "your bed might serve us well."

He sighed and the guilt over Demi passed a little.

"Why don't you sleep very well?" she said and turned the page. She tucked her legs in next to him on the bed.

He stroked her hair. "Too much on my mind."

"Have you always been restless?"

"Since I began pondering questions greater than myself."

"Like women?"

He rubbed her earlobe between a thumb and forefinger. "I suppose, and about the mysteries of being alive."

"How many women have you brought here?" she asked, turning her head to the room and back to him. The room was lushly appointed. A beige fur rug of camel's hair, a Rococo chair, a filigreed writing desk, a large fireplace. Enough room in the chamber for two.

"None."

A wry smile began at the corner of her mouth. "I'm not naive. I'm not the first."

"But you are."

"Not your first lover."

He drew in a long breath, and the fullness caused her to rise an inch on his abdomen. He held her there, pondering a response. "True, for most men my age."

She licked her index finger and turned another page. "How many others?"

"Several."

She dug her knees into his thighs. "How many?"

He stopped stroking her hair. "They're all in the past now."

"Then it won't matter if you share." The warmth of her skin beneath the loose gown neared a flashpoint.

"Why ruin the illusion that you're the one?" he asked. "You do believe me, don't you?"

"I want to understand," she said.

"My past sexual appetite or my moral corruption? The two went hand-in-hand."

"I want to see how many other women found you desirous."

The pressure of her body felt heavier over his. "And what could knowing this possibly accomplish?"

"To understand why my desire for you is so great."

He lifted a strand of her hair to his nose and breathed in the underlying message—she was falling, too. Using his better judgment, he rounded down. "I stopped counting after twenty-five."

She flipped a page. The colour rose on her neck.

"Could you name them all?"

A viper lay beneath her questions, so he stopped himself from teasing her. "Do you want me to?"

She glanced from the book to him. "I suppose not," then she injected the venom, "just the ones you were in love with."

He stopped her hand from turning another page. "Anne, enough."

"Does the heart ever say, 'Enough'?"

"Jealousy doesn't serve your heart well."

She tossed her hair back and rubbed his bare chest. Heat raced through him.

"I know you've deeply loved another," she said.

His confession to Father de Breuil bobbed to the surface, but Athos knocked the thought aside—that the priest would have divulged his secret. Anne was only flushing out his devotion. Irksome but also provocative.

"What difference does it make who I've loved before? After the last few days, how could anyone else matter?" He entwined his fingers in her hair, thinking of the way their bodies had entwined, scenes that surpassed the pillow book. "Of all of my lovers, you've been the greatest enchantress. *You.*"

"I believe you." Her gaze wandered back to the book. The next page opened to a *ménage a trois.* She dragged two fingers across the page. "And this? Have you tried this?"

He nabbed her fingers and brought them to his mouth for a kiss. "Everything but that."

"Would you?"

He had no reference point for the territory she was venturing into. "Your boundaries are limitless," he said and took her fingers into his mouth.

"Would you? For me?"

He slowly slipped her fingers from between his lips and rested her hand on his chest. "I want only one person."

"It wouldn't be about love," she said, inching up his body.

"Everything should be."

"So your answer is no."

"My answer is my body wants only you," he said.

"And what does my body want?"

Her suggestion touched every nerve. Part of him was titillated. Another part felt wrong. She was asking him to consider veering off his singular devotion to one, God's plan.

She put the book in front of him. "Doesn't this picture make your body quiver?"

Of course the threesome aroused him. Why wouldn't it?

"Anne," he said, closing the book and sliding it under the next pillow. "I'm a man. Obviously, the thought of three has crossed my mind, ever since the day I saw that picture. But I want one person to love. I've always wanted one. I don't need to be pleasured by more. I'm full with you. You alone are more than I need."

She crawled on top of him and gathered the night dress to her waist and straddled his hips. He ground his growing girth between the cheeks of her buttocks. He wanted her as much now as he had in the many previous days and nights of intense stimulation and consummation.

"Since I have no dowry," she said and removed the gown all the way, "then I must give you the only gift I have."

He wiggled out of his pants. She bucked at his immediate entry but engulfed him. Her body fuelled his fire. His body needed nothing but her, where the centre of his life had shifted.

•    •    •

She fell asleep in his arms around midnight. He covered her in the goose-down covers within the plush folds of his bed, which was the largest in the house, and he closed the canopy. After an hour of sleeplessness and reading, he decided to prepare them a bath.

Athos signalled his oldest servant, Zahn, by hanging a lantern at the double front doors. Zahn was the only one who had been instructed to stay behind at the gatehouse, and the old valet set about his orders to fill a small copper tub placed in the bedroom. Zahn, the former valet of Athos's father, was the only person infrequently allowed into Athos's private realm. An hour before dawn, the bath was ready. Anne had slept through the entire process.

Athos bathed first and soaked up the hottest temperatures. The steam rose, opening his lungs. His mind travelled from one end of his conscious life to the other. Had it been true he could name all his lovers? Yes. Each was a bloom on a rose bush. But he hadn't loved any with his heart. The only one to hold that coveted spot had been the one he had never made love to. *Will never make love to.* Demi's name floated up in the steam, and he submerged his head in the water, hoping to wash it away.

A half hour into his soak, Anne stirred. Athos wrapped a sheet around himself and gently woke her. Her eyes looked refreshed, bluer. Her beauty aroused him again, but he wanted her to enjoy the warm water, so he kissed the back of her hand and led her naked to the bath. She lowered herself in without persuasion.

He lay on the rug beside the tub and enjoyed the sound of her splashes and the soft expressions of her pleasure. For once, the peacefulness lulled him into a light sleep. Athos listened as Anne languished in the tub. She hummed and spoke. "Are you sleeping?"

In a half-dreaming state, he leaned up onto his elbows on the fur, stretched each leg, and crossed his ankles. The dewy sheet covered his bare body. He grabbed her ring finger as she extended her arm from the lukewarm water, and Athos exhaled. Or dreamed he did.

"I've heard it said that love is the most selfish of passions." His voice was velvet. "Stand for me."

A melody of dripping water accompanied her rise. The sheen of her skin matched the milk and lavender he'd added to the water. Damp tendrils clung to the nape of her neck, and droplets licked down her bosom. His dream, or reality, had finally delivered him paradise.

Her figure rekindled erotic scenes from their time together. Images of ecstasy flashed in his fluid thoughts. Every simple curve of her skin had been his secret to discover and plunder for all time.

He wandered in and out of the recent memories. He yearned to wake up or know if he was awake. He swung himself into the bath, where he stood and opened the sheet to her svelte body. Pressed together, he draped it around them before he let it fall. His hand wandered over her curves and indulged her peaks and valleys. His mouth and tongue took her collarbone, neck and breasts. He caressed her flushed cheeks.

"Do you love me?" The thought formed out of thin air from a distant place in his mind.

Not waiting for her response, he heard himself repeat the question between kisses on her body, a reed quivering in a pond. Water spilled from the tub as he eased down her length. Her breathing quickened, and her hands plunged into his hair. He knelt, up to his torso in water, and used the soaked sheet to pull her thighs closer. His exhales tickled her belly and caused her to quake.

Caught in the twilight phase of a dream, Athos looked up and witnessed a shining halo of light, brighter than the sun.

He gazed straight into the face of Demi.

"Fere? Fere?" Anne called.

Athos jerked his head off the rug and blinked at the blindspots in his vision. Strong morning light penetrated the windows.

"You finally fell asleep," Anne said, peering over the rim of the tub. "I take credit."

Athos attempted a half-smile and found his feet to stand. He staggered nude to the nearest armoire.

"Maybe you shouldn't get up so quickly," Anne said, her amusement barely disguised.

"I'll be fine," he murmured and opened a drawer filled with clean clothes. He quickly found a pair of pants and covered himself. He grabbed both doors of the armoire for support, to steady his breath, to erase Demi's lingering form. In a remote corner of his mind, he dug a burrow, buried her vision, and tamped down the dark ground.

"Fere? Are you feeling well?" Anne asked. The water splashed to indicate she was getting out.

Calming his nerves, he tried to collect himself. He rolled back his shoulders and put his hands in his front pockets. Inside one, his hand clenched the forgotten contents. In his right pocket, he felt Demi's handkerchief.

# The Past Returns

Anne's arms slid underneath his as he plunged the handkerchief deeper into its hiding place.

"You're cold," she said, rubbing her damp hands and forearms across the muscles tightening in his gut. "I think you should bathe again. With me."

"Not now," he said and slipped away from her, as if escaping an unsprung animal trap, a skill he and Bronte had perfected as reckless boys. He headed straight to the fireplace on the other end of the room.

A fire. A solution.

"Is that what I think it is?" she asked from across the room.

He quickly looked back at her, blanking his face of any possible guilt, to find her focused on the centre of the mantel.

She'd discovered the place where his family treasures were secured for safekeeping.

A rectangular casket, made of rustic oak and inlaid bronze, rested on the mantel between two tall silver candlesticks. He hadn't touched the safe since he'd removed his mother's ring. Like that heirloom, the contents of the casket were worth more than any price they could bring from an interested buyer. The antique pieces, gold, silver, and jewelled trinkets, told the history of his family and were kept with the papers documenting his lineage. He occasionally reviewed the casket's contents out of reverence. Handling them meant touching his own past.

In the present, they gave him an immediate opportunity to rid himself of the potential disaster in his pocket.

"Here." He brought it down and gestured for her. "You must know your family now."

From a chair near the hearth, she threw a blanket around her shoulders and approached him as if she'd been given the map to a secret passageway. With steady hands, she took the box and sat in the chair. She studied the latch.

"The lock's broken," he said. "Just lift it."

She complied. Her eyes scanned the contents, as greedily as he had as a youngster. He hoped she would study each piece in detail and give him a short window to clandestinely burn the handkerchief.

He built a fire with unequaled efficiency. Every move mattered. Within minutes, a fire crackled and shot up the flue. He squatted by the flames, and the heat stung his thighs and knees. He looked back once to check if Anne was still preoccupied. She'd found his mother's droplet pearl necklace.

"It suits you," he said. His hand dove for the handkerchief.

Anne spun the pearls around her fingers and wrists and lifted them against the light from the fire. "Your family has more wealth than the church of England." She giggled at her exaggeration.

He nodded involuntarily, while his thoughts tumbled. He turned his face to the fire and stood unnaturally still. Inside his pocket, he wadded the cloth. Closing his eyes, he removed his fist and pressed it hard into his chest. He bunched the cloth tighter and tighter and dug his knuckles into his breastbone. A hot wave of air took his breath, and the fire flushed his face.

*I can't burn it.*

The reason escaped him. It represented forbidden territory. Blame. Star-crossed pain. Ramming his fist back into his pocket, shame coursed up him. Feet apart, he grabbed the mantel to block more of Anne's view of his guilty face. He prayed to God his weak heart would never be exposed.

"Anne," he finally called out, still facing the heat, "I need to leave for an hour or two. Do you mind?"

She hummed a note or two that he interpreted as complete distraction. From the rapture on her face and the glint of jewels in her eyes, Athos judged the timing was right. He kissed Anne's forehead, dressed quickly, and left the château, debating which direction made the most sense to take care of one loose detail.

•     •     •

Bronte's father, Jean Claude, opened his magistrate's office to Athos after the third knock. Typically a large man, he was drooping. A great force seemed to have battered his characteristic authority. Brown circles caused the skin underneath his eyes to sag, and his shoulders hung like a lame animal. Remembering Father Luc's plea to help Jean Claude, Athos feared he had arrived too late.

"Have you news of Bronte?" Athos asked, a few steps inside the office.

Jean Claude nodded in the direction of an interior door, which led to the family's residence. The door opened, and Bronte emerged in riding clothes and dusty boots.

Athos startled in surprise. With open arms, he rushed across the room to his friend, only to be met by a glacial stare. Bronte crossed his arms over his chest.

Athos paused in mid-stride, wind-whipped and confused.

"Thank the saints you're alive," Athos said after a few seconds of silence. He stuck out his hand, and Bronte shook it half-heartedly. "You're back."

"And you're married." Bronte's flat expression didn't cover the snide tone. Patches of sunburn covered his skin, and his dark hair flipped wildly at the sides of his face, evidence of a long, hard ride.

"Did you just arrive?" Athos turned back to read the face of Jean Claude, who emptied his lungs of a ragged breath.

"Only just," Jean Claude said.

"Father," Bronte said, "leave us. Let me tell him."

In passing, Jean Claude landed a heavy hand on Athos's shoulder then exited the office without a word.

"Tell me what?" Athos asked. "Your father looks ill and you ... where have you been?"

"I didn't want anyone to know where I was or what I was doing."

"And what were you doing? You never sent a single letter. Everything's happened since you left." Athos sat on the edge of a nearby desk, which was drowning in papers and scrolls. "Your father has been sick with worry, as have I."

"You?" Bronte cocked an eyebrow. "The rumours high and low are that you've closed yourself off with your new wife, shuttered yourselves in the château. The entire province says you've relinquished everything for her."

"Relinquished?" The word irritated the back of Athos's throat. "You're the one who left without a word. You didn't say good-bye, much less leave a tender note to your one true love."

"You and your insipid poetry!" Bronte flung several papers from the desk into the air. "It won't do you any good now. You've gone and married a woman darker than this—" and Bronte briefly snatched Athos's ink-stained finger.

"She's a survivor," Athos said on the verge of shouting. "And if you'd been so concerned about me, why leave? You knew my intentions were to marry her. You probably ran off because you couldn't stand seeing us together." He threw up his hands. "What else could it be?"

"It's about the truth." As coolly as Bronte spoke, he filched Demi's handkerchief from Athos's gaping pocket.

Instinctively, Athos shot out a hand. Bronte snapped the handkerchief away and backed up. He carefully held the square up to a window and the white stitching of a **D** stood out. Bronte dropped his chin and narrowed his eyes. He gripped the handkerchief and pumped his fist above his head.

"Libertine!"

"That's a mistake," Athos said, his lungs a desert.

"Like the gloves?" Bronte shook the handkerchief until he trembled. "Like the gloves?!"

"I'm here to set this right," Athos said. "I came to demand that your father marry you to Demi and not to someone you don't love."

Bronte threw the handkerchief on the floor. "Your title can't solve *this* problem!"

In a run, Bronte slammed his shoulder into Athos's chest. The impact sent the two backward over the table and onto the floor. A wooden floorboard cracked beneath them, and Bronte raged on, straddling Athos and landing punches. He kneed Athos in the sides and growled and grunted in hatred and misery. Athos blocked the blows but didn't return them. He deserved his just rewards, if only this once.

Bronte cocked him in the jaw, and Athos tasted blood on his tongue.

"I'm not done yet," Bronte said and picked them both off the floor. He swung Athos by the front of his shirt and began shoving him toward the door.

"Did you ask this seductress you now call your wife," Bronte said and shoved, "how she knew your weakness for poetry?" Another shove. "And wine?" A final shove. "And *God!*"

Athos caught Bronte's upper arms. The two wrestled until they fell to the floor. Athos, on all fours, scrambled to his knees for some dignity and a semblance of reason. "Stop this," Athos spat out. "Whatever you're implying, stop it!"

Bronte rolled over on his back and, between heaves of air, refused the truce. "The Shakespeare didn't work on me." He laughed sarcastically. "Ah, but the honeysuckle in her hair? Now that did *me* in."

Athos felt as if he'd been punched in the gut, and the last of his even temper evaporated.

"No!" Athos throttled Bronte and sank his thumbs into his neck, unable to fend off images of Bronte with Anne. Athos squeezed tighter, embittered that Bronte may have sampled all her pleasures. His face reddening, Bronte kicked and clawed in a losing battle with Athos's blackness.

"Stop," Bronte gasped.

But Athos couldn't. He overflowed with rage. Bronte's lips began to turn blue.

Bronte wheezed. "She's not who she seems."

Sweat dripped from Athos's forehead and onto his hands and fingers. He let it slip his stranglehold. Athos fell to the side, but relief didn't come. He flung over and pinned Bronte down again, pushing out the little air he had left.

"Whatever you know could never erase what you've done with her." Athos seethed through his teeth. "Meet me in the square an hour before dusk. Bring your sword."

Tasting blood again, Athos left before Bronte could regain his voice.

# A Musketeer's Privilege

The rumoured duel pitted friend against friend, brother against brother, in the midst of the Fête de Vin, the province's late summer festival of wine-making. By dusk, villagers clogged every corner of the centre of Blois, doubling the festival's usual attendance. Athos pushed his way into the crowd armed with the best sword in his possession. Whispers swirled around him in a winding hiss. Every age and station were represented. Athos gripped the pommel of the naked blade, a foreign object compared to Anne's body.

After challenging Bronte to the duel, Athos had returned home to find that she had left Valliere to visit her brother, according to her note by the casket of family treasures. Athos had been relieved she was gone so he didn't have to explain why he needed a sword. Her absence also gave him time to decide how to broach the subject of her dalliance with Bronte.

*A dalliance!*

How could it have happened? How could God have let it? Of course, he blamed Bronte and his un-gentlemanly ways. Bronte knew Athos was interested in her and that she was not pure, making his motives less than clean. Anne, on the other hand, may not have known of Athos's affections and was tempted before he could divulge them. Whether or not Anne was the instigator, Bronte had betrayed him, and his insult required a response, possibly a deadly one.

*"Bronte! Show yourself!"* Athos's outburst silenced the murmurs in the village centre and left only the sound of the festival flags flapping in a brisk wind.

Men and women glanced behind each other and back to Athos as he paced a line of retreating onlookers. People gawked from stalls of festival goods, and colourfully dressed street performers trained their eyes on him. This was the first closeup glimpse many of his subjects had ever gotten of their new sovereign. Part of him wanted to show strength, if their opinion of him was as Bronte had said— weakened by desire.

From three deep in the crowd, a woman's voice arose. "Is it true you wish Bronte to marry Demi?"

He'd heard the voice before and thanked God it wasn't Demi's. But whose?

The mass of bodies parted, and Margot walked out into the open.

"I asked: Do you wish Bronte to marry Demi rather than me?" Her jaw set.

"Where did you hear this?" Athos demanded, and cast a stern stare at her and the blank faces in the crowd.

"Racine." Margot smiled smugly.

Athos grumbled the name of Bronte's brother to himself and stalked from one end of the crowd to the other in search of the culprit.

"You won't find him here," Margot said, a hand on her hip. "He's gone to claim Demi for himself, since his brother will soon be dead."

Athos spun on his heels and headed straight for Margot, whose back stiffened at the oncoming force.

"You're shameless!" he blurted within inches of her face.

"Me?" She laughed from the belly. "I've only had my sights set on one, unlike someone we know."

"I'll remind you," he said and jutted his index finger under her chin, "that as long as you're in this province, you're here at my pleasure. Overstep your place, and exile shall be yours."

Flushed, Margot raised her chin off the tip of his finger and forced herself to curtsy.

"Leave her alone."

Athos whirled around to find Bronte in the widening circle of people. His sword was drawn and a single line of sweat ran down one temple.

"You have no idea what you've done," Bronte said, shaking his head.

Athos studied the hard lines on Bronte's face. His eyes were unforgiving and mouth, downturned.

"You disavowed me the day you touched my wife," Athos said.

"She wasn't your wife then and shouldn't be now."

"I could kill you for that insult," Athos said. "Among others."

Athos drew his sword and waved it to clear a larger area. Several peasants cried in fear and cowered.

"Put away your sword and hear me out," Bronte said.

"Why? I love her, and you can't change that."

"She doesn't love you. She only wants your wealth. It's all she's ever been after."

"Oh and I should believe the man who showed no restraint for what wasn't his?" Athos pointed his sword directly at Bronte's chest. "A black heart doesn't deserve forgiveness."

"I didn't come here expecting it," Bronte said and poised *engarde*.

In response, Athos flashed his blade high, and for a moment, the two stood immobile, absorbing the gravity of their unbending egos.

Athos lunged. His aggression scattered the crowd around the periphery. A few ran into alleys. Bronte parried and riposted. The clink of their blades sounded off the granite front of the cathedral. Surrounded by the church and several rows of multi-story shops, the street became an echo chamber.

Never before had Athos used his full skills on his sparring partner. Today was different. Every past frustration between them was on trial. Every petty disagreement, all of Bronte's jealousy, each word of Athos's overwrought advice, congealed in the fight at hand. Before, their fencing had served as practice, attempts to even the scales. Now, the stakes were death.

Unleashing his restraint, Athos rained Bronte with skilful attacks, each more technical than the last. Bronte lost ground and fell farther and farther back toward a vat of crushed grapes in the street. A worried wine-maker flung his arms around the wooden rim and guarded his season's harvest. Bronte's blocks held, but Athos kept the upper hand.

"You're bewitched," Bronte said, struggling for air at a break in Athos's surges. "You're fighting the messenger. If you kill me, you'll never know the truth."

Athos pointed his sword at his opponent and swished the blade between them. "I'm not sure I'd believe your truth."

The two exchanged several rounds of attacks and skirted around the wooden vat while ignoring the uneasy vintner who squalled and shook his fists.

The barrel between them, Bronte leaned over the edge to catch his breath. "She wants to isolate you. Once she does, she gets what she wants."

Athos chopped at the thick oak side near Bronte's head.

"Fight!" Athos shouted. "You don't deserve mercy."

"I'm not the one you should be fighting," Bronte said and stood up but returned his sword to his belt. Athos leaped into the vat and pulled Bronte in by the lapels. They slipped and fell sideways in the knee-deep mash of grapes. Athos lost control of his sword and began punching until they were both covered in pulp.

Villagers encircled the barrel and grew more appalled at each punch of their sovereign. Bronte shielded himself rather than fight, which caused Athos's anger to grow. The crowd jeered at Athos and cheered on Bronte, the man in control of his emotions. Bronte was winning by staying composed.

"His honour is in question!" Athos spiralled in several di-rections and yelled at the judging crowd. Athos caught the eyes of a taller cloaked figure on the steps of the cathedral, and the man's piercing gaze reminded Athos of Father de Breuil's. "Bronte's an insatiable satyr who has defamed your new comtesse."

A growl came from behind, and Bronte clamped Athos in a choke hold, which caused him to drop his sword. The two fell to their knees in the barrel. Athos clawed at Bronte's forearm and spotted his sword, partially sunk in the grapes.

"Listen to me!" Bronte snarled in Athos's ear and tightened his hold. "I know things about Anne that you don't. I need to tell you, but not here. Look at your subjects. They think you've gone mad, and from the looks of you, I agree."

Athos scanned the disappointed stares. For once, he understood the meaning of disgrace. It heaped new hurt on top of old. The shame and the losses—of his father, priest, Demi— collided at once. Anne seemed to be his only foothold.

"Release me," Athos demanded as the hilt of his sword almost submerged.

"Promise me you'll come to your senses and hear me out," Bronte said.

Athos nodded and Bronte let go. The two, covered in blue and purple grape skins, stood. For a moment, the crowd released a collective sigh until Athos kicked the hilt of his sword into his hand, whipped around, and thrust. His sword entered Bronte's shoulder. Silence claimed the street.

Bronte fell to his knees and clutched the cut with his blotchy glove. The colour in his face drained away, blood streaked his shirt, and he sat hard in the mash. Athos stared at the tip of his bloody sword, and an unexpected emptiness grew inside him.

"Your eyes," Bronte said. "She's beguiled you."

Feral at the hands of fate, Athos saw no choice but to follow through, to resolutely counter the rumours of his weakness. He raised his sword and aimed for Bronte's heart. Women shrieked in terror, and the crowd whipped into a near panic around the vat. Athos trained his eyes on target and the white noise between his ears drowned out the wild sounds, including his own conscience.

Then metal slammed his sword and broke his aim. Athos's wrist twisted in pain but he held onto his weapon. From one side of the barrel, a shiny, clean blade nudged into his armpit.

"Drop your weapon if you want to keep your fencing arm," Father Luc said. His voice boomed above the stunned crowd.

Athos looked the menacing blade up and down, from his arm to the strong grip of Father Luc's. The priest's solemn stare underscored his lethal intent.

"Stay out of this!" Athos took a step back, but the tip of Father Luc's sword stayed put.

"You forced me to get involved," Father Luc said and tipped his head at the sword Athos clung to. "I never gave you permission to use my sword to kill a man."

Athos gulped and squeezed the pommel of the borrowed weapon. He hadn't been able to resist commandeering it from Father Luc's collection for the duel. This one was by far the most impressive. The value of the silver inlay on the gold hilt would have fed an entire village for a year.

"Hand it over," Father Luc said, "and tend to Bronte's wound. Then pay the grower for his grapes."

Athos hesitated. Bronte eyelids drooped. Athos released the sword into the vat and snatched a cheese cloth from an outstretched hand in the crowd. He quickly wrapped Bronte's shoulder and handed the sword over to its owner.

"Lift him," Father Luc said, standing down. "And get him inside at once."

·   ·   ·

Soliciting a few villagers to help the three inside the church, Father Luc situated Bronte on a comfortable bench in his study.

The priest focused on stabilising Bronte. With his head and shoulder elevated, Bronte never lost consciousness. Father Luc tucked a blanket around him while Athos let the reality of his actions soak in. Athos found a pitcher of water and offered a drink. Bronte refused it. Their clothes, boots, gloves were blotchy with juice and the remnants of pulp.

"He needs tea and time," the priest said, and as he spoke a helper appeared with a warm cup of chamomile and an armful of healing ointments.

Athos rubbed his face and tried to erase the evening's outcome. "Did you hear—?"

"About why you two were duelling? Who hasn't." Father Luc didn't bother to look up from the patient.

"Not from me," Bronte snapped. "I'd barely had time to get off my horse when he picked a fight."

After assessing the damage, Father Luc dug through a nearby shelf of white altar vestments and table runners used for sacrament and began ripping them into strips. "We'll have to use these. How deep was the cut?"

"I don't know. It didn't hit bone," Athos said, thinking, *I didn't hit bone. I, the man responsible.* He glanced at Bronte, whose pale face was upturned to the light from the window above the bench. Athos read his friend's expression not as painful but as a man tortured by circumstance. Same for him. Both God-forsaken and debased by ego.

Athos leaned against the wall farthest from the bench and watched the priest wind a new dressing on top of the first soaked bandage.

"What's his prognosis, monseigneur Musketeer?" Athos instantly regretted his sarcastic tone.

"If I can get this bandage tight enough," Father Luc said, pulling it snug despite Bronte's squints, "he'll heal faster. A shoulder wound is an annoyance but most often not a death sentence."

Athos carefully observed how the priest treated the wound and remembered his father showing him similar techniques, for future occasions in battle, not lovers' tiffs.

*Am I wrong to be angry?* Anger still lurked in his thoughts.

"Can you rest?" Father Luc asked Bronte once his wound was redressed.

"No." Bronte's voice remained strong.

"So I gather neither of you learned a lesson." Father Luc glared briefly in Athos's direction. "Come out of the shadows, Comte. You've been spending far too much time in them."

Athos dragged himself to the middle of the room. Bronte finally cast him a look, though it was dripping with contempt.

"Let's hear it then," Father Luc said turning from one stone wall to the other. "Don't make me pull out my sword again to drag the story out of you two."

"I thought you gave me all your weapons," Athos said sourly.

"I always keep a spare behind the pulpit." Father Luc chuckled to himself.

"If you hadn't, I'd be dead," Bronte said and sneered at Athos, who advanced a step.

"You defiled my wife."

"Still blaming me, I see," Bronte huffed.

"You wanted her from the very beginning. Why I couldn't see that before ..."

The priest held Athos by the waist to prevent another step. "Leave it. That's over."

"I'll never forget," Athos said.

"You take everything for granted," Bronte started. "The way you treat me, your subjects, because of your wealth and privilege, you just can't see beyond yourself. Have you any idea the repercussions of your mistake with Demi? She won't even see me. I left Berry because I cared about you, and as a result, my chance for happiness is swept away."

Athos's laughter filled the room. "You left her! You sought the charms of others. *Of Anne.* How is Demi supposed to react?"

Bronte grimaced trying to sit up but the pain kept him down. "Anne has motives I believe are false. She used me as a way to get to you, Athos. Granted, I was easy. She knew my eye was tantalised by her, and she exploited my weakness. But there was something that wasn't right about her. About her *and* her brother."

"Of course, drag him into it," Athos said and threw his arms up. "Blame everyone but yourself."

"They weren't *right* together," Bronte said.

"Careful," Father Luc warned, his mouth a thin line. "I'm obliged by my orders to counsel you against false accusations. The church is known to exercise extreme vengefulness."

"That's why it was important for me to act quickly," Bronte said. "After Anne and I were together, it struck me. The way she and her brother held their bodies in each other's presence. Their looks at one another. The small touches. They weren't right. They seemed to behave as if they were lovers."

Athos shook his head vigorously, trying to throw off the doubts.

"That's when I knew I had to find out more," Bronte said, rubbing his forehead. "She was already starting to lose interest in me, and I knew you were next."

"There was no next victim," Athos said bitterly. "You only felt jealous, of her brother, of me."

"No, it was more than jealousy. I went straight to Paris and started searching for anyone who knew them in the church or at Court."

"I've run across no one in the priesthood," Father Luc added.

"Despite their stature, they leave no trace," Bronte nodded. "But I did find a valet, one who said he'd worked for Anne's brother a short time in Paris. And that's how I discovered they'd known about you for a while."

"She's driven you to the edge of madness," Athos said, shaking his head at both men.

"She saw us, Athos. You and me. She saw us in Paris after the death of your father, when we were caught up in the blur of parties and beautiful women and wine, and you were a mess, so why would you suspect we were being watched, unless she wanted you to know? She was calculating and hunting."

"I can't believe this!" Athos shouted at Father Luc and pointed at Bronte. "Give him something for the delirium."

"Just listen to me. The valet said the brother and sister were as I described, too close to seem platonic but not blatantly a couple in public. He told me they were trying to position themselves to gain a parish in a province where a new sovereign had taken over. This sovereign had just lost his father. Think about it. She could have been everywhere in Paris that we were."

"I would have remembered her, and you would have, too. She's too conspicuous."

"And sly if she wants to be. So I asked around about her, talking to any courtier I knew."

"You mean you went to visit all the women you bedded," Athos said sardonically.

Bronte rolled his eyes. "On this trip—*for you*—I was as chaste as you were before your ludicrous wedding, and my instincts were correct. Several of my friends described a woman in Paris at that time who fits Anne's description. But she wasn't gregarious or interested in entanglements or making a show. If anything, they said, she seemed aloof—and prone to memorising every detail about you and me."

"That proves nothing, except that you'll go to extreme lengths to ruin the name of the new comtesse of Berry. You don't have proof! None of this sways me. It only makes me believe the affair you had with her hurt you."

"She's blinded you!" Bronte raised himself to sitting. He steadied his bad shoulder and moaned. "There's more to this story. I knew the information from Paris wasn't enough. It felt like only the start. The valet urged me to find the enclave of Jesuits in England where de Breuil had supposedly studied."

"Did you find it?" Father Luc questioned and went to Bronte's side to encourage him to lie back down. Bronte wouldn't have it.

"After several weeks, I did," he nodded up at the priest. "In the south, a small order knew them, under different names but by the same physical descriptions. The order had expelled de Breuil for inappropriate behaviour with a novice and punished her for stealing from the coffers. After they were expelled from the enclave, the Jesuits realised the two had taken enough valuables to live abroad as nobles, at least for a while."

"Your trip to England explains why we didn't hear from you." Father Luc dragged himself to his desk chair and slumped into it. "If all you say is true ..."

"None of it's true!" Athos fumed with the same anger that had almost strangled and stabbed his friend to death. "Where's the proof? There's none! Only vague connections."

"The Jesuits also believed this couple had poisoned the priest who discovered them in bed together, trying to silence him. The poor man confessed about what he saw before he died." Bronte dropped his head. His chest caved in, seemingly because of a single sob. "He died of the same symptoms as Father Turre."

The room spun. Under a wave of incredulity, Athos stumbled for the study door. He couldn't look at Bronte, couldn't hear any more, couldn't understand why Anne had induced such hatred. Her rejection of Bronte had sent him on a wild chase. Now poison filled the air.

"You're wrong," Athos said, hearing a crack in his defence though his loyalty was indescribable.

"You risk everything if I'm not," Bronte warned.

"She's lived through incredible suffering. Her heart is true." But his declarations began to sound hollower and hollower.

Father Luc called out. "Are there any signs or clues to confirm Bronte's story?"

Athos bunched the front of his shirt into a tight fist. "Until you've both come to your senses, stay away from Valliere."

As soon as Athos appeared outside the cathedral, the crowd whispered for a minute then fell silent. He walked down the centre of the street and returned the quiet stares of his subjects. He stopped and threw coins at the feet of the hapless vintner and moved on. At the end of the gauntlet, he took two bottles of wine from a timid merchant and escorted himself home.

# 25

# Light and Dark

Zahn met Athos at the gatehouse of Valliere and proclaimed that the wedding gift for Anne had arrived. "She's quite taken with it," the dutiful old servant said.

Athos asked Zahn to take his horse for safety's sake. Introducing his horse to the new Arabian stallion he'd purchased for Anne could wait. Zahn obliged and excused himself for the night.

The arrival of the Arabian had been delayed because Athos's arrangements had fallen to the wayside in the rush up to the wedding. On his way to the stables, he hoped his present might soften the conversation he was about to initiate. Bronte's accusations hung like a fog on his conscience. Athos wished he could burn the mists of doubt from his mind. But until he could clear the air with Anne, the claims would cloud their future.

Anne stood in the center of the stable yard and petted the snout of the yellow Arabian, a perfect match to her cream-coloured dress. He had wanted to own the breed for years, and his new wife had given him a good reason to finally buy one. The horse shook its head and mane vainly. The creature's pride befitted its new owner—Anne could never live less than a full-blooded life.

"What do you think?" Athos called to her from the fence. There was a sad tinge to his voice, which he couldn't hide.

She looked over and her shining eyes turned quizzical. "What happened to your clothes?"

In his bewilderment, he had completely forgotten about the grape stains. He blinked and shook his head a little at his appearance.

"The Fête de Vin," he said, almost to himself.

"And I wasn't invited?" She *tsk-tsked* and snapped her fingers. "Do you need reminding so soon of my place by your side?"

He fought to return her smile and ducked through the fencing to join her. The stallion angled between them, sniffed Athos's purple shoulder and reversed direction for a clump of grass by her feet.

"See," she said, "even the horse knows where the grass is greener."

"How was your brother?" Athos said, watching for any reaction, wanting to wash himself of Bronte's sacrilegious story of the two.

She continued to gaze at the magnificent horse, and a twinkle of wanderlust filled her eyes. Athos grabbed her hand and focused her attention on him.

"Are you happy here?" he asked. "With me?"

He yearned for the intense feelings between them to patch Bronte's wounds.

She peered deeply into his eyes. "Something has happened."

He nodded once and squeezed her hands. "Bronte's home."

Her chest rose and fell in an acknowledging sigh. "What is he to us now?"

"Unhappy."

She tried to take her hands from his. He kept hold.

"He's jealous," she said.

"I don't know what to think."

Anne sighed again but in frustration. "You made the decision to marry me without him. He's not the number one person in your life anymore."

"It's more serious." Athos held in a breath before finishing. "He claims you and he were lovers."

Anne growled low in her throat, and she tried to free her hands again. "And whose story do you want?"

"I don't want a story. I want the truth." Athos searched her face for a clue. None came.

"I love you," she said, her body suddenly against his. "We love each other. I feel it."

She slipped her hands to the back of his neck, rigid with tension.

"Who am I to believe, Anne?" He strove to sound even-keeled, but he wanted the knot of blame untied. "Him or you?"

"What do you want to believe?" she asked, clutching his shoulders. "I can't live up to your ideals, but I told you the truth about myself before we were married."

Athos tried to shrug her off, but she held on tightly. He looked away to hide the hurt building inside.

"Yes," Anne said, her breath warm on his earlobe. "Bronte and I were together. Once."

He squeezed his eyes shut. Her candour was a dark secret shared to a condemned man. Black thoughts washed over him. *Why, God? Why? Why Bronte?* The thought stuck to his tongue until he blurted it out, which caused the stallion to prance in an erratic pattern.

"Why Bronte?" A beggar might have asked for food less pitifully.

"Why?" she repeated in a whisper across his neck. "To find out about you."

*No!* More than anything, he wanted Bronte to be a complete liar. More than the contrast of black to white, more than the certainty of light giving way to dark.

"I immediately regretted it," she said. "He made it difficult to break from him."

He had to see her eyes. Their blue streaks cut a thousand tiny slices into his thin skin; their truth seemed crystal clear.

"He wanted more, and you said no?" Athos pressed.

"Yes." Behind her at the fence, the stallion pawed the ground and whinnied. "Our one encounter made him go insane."

Athos understood this detail personally. His own sanity poised on a splintered rock about to sheer. Too much hinged on her answers. To side with her meant disbelieving, even forsaking, his friend and possibly his priest.

Athos's temples pounded. "You didn't have to be with him to find out about me."

"He demanded an exchange. Information about you for ..." She looked down. "A woman with my past has little virtue to preserve."

"You could have said no to him and come to me. I wanted as much. Couldn't you see that?"

"It's so easy for noblemen." Anne threw her shoulders back. "Your fortunes aren't tied to virtue or caprice. Women live by a different set of standards. My stolen innocence can't be returned, and some might argue there's a certain freedom once it's gone."

He recognised her stance as that of a warrior preparing for battle. Her walls were rising again. Scaling them a second time would be an epic feat. He gathered her hands and dug deeply for empathy.

"The abuse you suffered was tragic, but you cannot let it define you. You shouldn't have let it this time."

"Fere, you know who I am. You fell in love with me anyway." She grabbed his wrists. "I'm changed because of you. Have faith in me as you have faith in God. A pious man, above all else, believes beyond question. Place me before all else."

Anne asked of him the greatest devotion he'd ever given, and his past transgressions flashed before him—Demi's handkerchief, their kiss, his misplaced heart. He assured himself it was all in the past. "I'll hold you sacred, if you belong only to me."

She rested her head on his chest and focused on his lips. "And God shall reward you."

Swallowing back his heartbeat, he nodded.

# Athos's Log, Near the Dawn of Darkness

*Bronte will have me believe Anne harbours the Devil. Yet I stand by my choice to love, to be condemned by it, if need be. I do not seek mercy. But I do seek forgiveness. God, forgive me for loving Demi. I know I must not see her ever again. Today, my heart says farewell. And one day, my mind will be free.*

# Desperate Oblivion

That night in his bedroom, Anne gave Athos several gifts. Surprised, he accepted a trio of fine wines from Avignon and a crude silver cuff. She slipped the piece high on his arm, between his underarm and triceps, and admired its perfect fit. She declared it, "A reminder of me."

He draped her with a new fox-trimmed cape and announced he'd prepared a night for them outside. Donning a light coat, he led her out into the late summer night, past the horse pastures and the new stallion, past the fenced border of his meadow, into a thick, indigo woods on a strip of his land. Their clothes rustled in the open air of the elemental grandeur around them. Oak and birch towered and swayed. Vines wove under their feet. A bevy of quail startled. He grabbed her small hand and pulled her toward a glow in the dense trees—a tall, square tent. Two oil lamps on poles illuminated the outside and candlelight flickered within the canvas walls.

Athos parted the tent flaps for her entrance. He had designed the getaway to escape. There, he intended to rediscover her body until his mind was numb.

"My lady," he said and bowed.

Inside the tight enclosure, his instructions to Zahn had been followed exactly. On one side, a sturdy butcher block table offered food, and on the other, a pallet of goose-down blankets and pillows billowed atop a jute rug.

She spun around twice in the centre of the space. Her silk skirt flared, and the cape rippled behind her. Her complicated sensual past, her beauty, her taste for the risqué, soaked his heart in the necessary tonic he craved—eroticism.

"I love it," she said, pink-cheeked from walking and spinning, "as much as I love you."

He unhooked her cape and threw it to the pallet. With a flourish, he twirled her toward the fresh feast on the table. Over her shoulder, he could see everything from her point of view. The candles, a loose bouquet of wildflowers, petite cutting boards spread with samples of savoury dried meats, sweet dates, and sugared orange rind, bread, and cheese. He nestled into her back and inhaled the moment.

"Hungry?" he asked, more guttural than sensual.

She nodded. Behind her, as if his hands were hers, he tore chunks of baguette and pinched hunks of cheese and fed them to her. She tipped her head to one side to take the food, and after each bite, he kissed her neck. On his lips, the salt of her skin cleansed his bitter palate. The hateful circumstances and misfortunes were replaced by the flavour of lust.

"Why here?" she asked, chewing lightly and leaning into his kisses.

"To be perfectly alone." He bit her ear eagerly. The screech of an owl interrupted his next kiss.

"You want to commune with the beasts. You're attracted to their freedom, like the stallion," she smiled, "like me."

"I hunt the wild." On his next kiss, he nipped her skin.

"And what shall you hunt tonight?" And she swivelled around so her lips met his.

Their kiss deepened. The food and her delicious tongue—dual flavours of skin and salt—were a sensual elixir. He craved no other remedy. Whether good or evil, she had to be his to make him forget. God offered no substitute. Or perhaps, God chose to look the other way.

Ravenously, savagely, he took her first on the table. He didn't bother undressing them. Their jostling spilled most of the food to the floor. Poised on the table's edge, she wrapped her legs around his waist and he stood. Between them, her skirt billowed into a silk cloud that he plundered to find the cure he required. He buried himself into her heat. Every pinprick of accusations from the last few days was deadened by each surge inside her. The candlesticks toppled and splattered wax on the canvas walls. *Let them burn*, Athos's body told Anne's. His momentum intensified and their flesh ignited. Her mouth issued throaty urges that stoked the blaze. Within moments, he raged them into oblivion.

To savour the aftermath, he stayed inside her. The flames of the fallen candles died, and the lanterns outside illuminated their entwined bodies in softness. Face to face, they unwound from the pinnacle of satisfaction. Each of their ragged, hot breaths slowed time. Then he withdrew and moved her to the respite of the bed.

"You act starved," she said, stretching out so that the blankets surrounded her like a thumb print in dough. She began untying her bodice, his eyes trained on her every motion.

"I just need to be with you." He shivered privately as he spoke and felt more desperate and needy than at any time in her presence.

She continued to undress for him and made sounds more sublime than carefully crafted poetry. The audible and visual stimuli stirred his most base desires. Unexpectedly, one desire was to control her, but the paradox of having her was also knowing he could never completely *have* her.

She lay naked among the puff of linens staring at him. His eyes wandered to her black armband.

"Will you ever take it off?" he asked, daring to touch it. His new cuff seemed the same width.

"No." She touched the silver on his arm. "I hope you'll honour me by always wearing yours."

"Does your brother mourn this way?" It tumbled out of him before he could reconsider.

"No." She turned toward him on her side so that the black band was hidden in the folds of blankets.

He exhaled. "I'm sorry."

Her mischievous look returned. "What part of me do you love the most?"

"Here," he whispered across her throat, "where your heartbeat echoes."

She wiggled closer, and he accepted her body's invitation. He placed his hands and the soft hair on his arms anywhere on Anne that provoked a pleasurable coo. Soon, he concentrated on the universe between her legs. Her thighs had a milky smoothness that made even his sovereign hands seem rough. Rarely had the women he'd known unfurled themselves as she did now. She nodded and he stroked. Her sighs cued him to concentrate his touch on the right spots to peak her pleasure. There and there. In and around. Until she bloomed. After a long, timeless stretch, he'd managed to give Anne several rounds of release, fiery and vocal.

In satisfied repose, she pulled his shirt over his head so that they lay naked together. "You would do anything for me," she said.

The thought occurred to him that he might. What more could she ask of him? She'd already challenged his moral and mental fortitude. He laughed a little. "You seem so sure."

She stood. The muted light from the lanterns danced across her bare body. She strolled to the door, opened the flap, and motioned outside. Before he could speak, she slipped out.

On his feet, goosebumps covered his entire body. He heard her shuffle quickly through the brush near the tent, and he lunged for the exit.

Just outside the door, the gaslight lit a bright bubble several feet wide. No sign of her. He'd never truly been naked with a woman outside before. He'd run naked as a boy and dipped in the lake without clothes but not with a woman. Once, he'd fondled a maid in a livery. But his parochial sexual history had favoured the ordinary. Now his nerves tingled with excitement, and he quickly dashed in the direction of her footfalls.

Outside the safety of the lantern light, the moon lit the woods in pale grey. He spotted the soft white backside of Anne, who hopped from clear patch to clear patch under the tree canopy. He thought he heard her laughing. It made him dizzy, the feeling of fresh air on his aroused body, a primal experience he'd never known.

*Am I on the verge of paradise? To experience Eden on Earth?*

He caught up, or she let him. It didn't matter. In the instant they touched, full body, he would, as she had claimed, do anything for her. He wanted to do everything to her. She was the fount of pleasure and knowledge granted to him by God.

Their bodies exchanged heat. They kissed sloppily and clung hip-to-hip. She made him feel bestial and want to mimic the wild woods that was their backdrop. He—a man. She—a woman. One—in the garden. She'd drawn him out to mate and find freedom from careful boundaries. His body and mind embraced the brazen invitation.

Neither led the other. She moved. He moved. Down to the bed of moss beneath them. Her on all fours. Him inside her. Their union evolved in reverse—from the sacred to the carnal. Their voices transformed into grunts. They surrendered to basic, physical need.

*Blood of my blood. Flesh of my flesh.*

Athos gave primitively of himself and took from her. They discovered the wild within the other and tumbled over the precipice of control. They unlocked the secret to the other side. Sweaty and full of raw sensation, they fell in a heap on the cool ground. The ordinary had been trampled. Catechism, Godliness, temperance, virtue. In the vast solitude of the forest, he believed his body had been existentially altered. Indeed, his mind had been.

•    •    •

The chill in the air eventually drove them back to the tent and the comfort of the pallet. In the passing hours, the forest grew quieter. His senses, on the other hand, grew keener. He believed the nature of their lovemaking had crossed a threshold. She thrived outside of the norm, and she desired him to leap over.

Lying languidly on top of him, she studied his face. "You're thinking deeply."

"I'll never have enough of you," he said and cupped her buttocks.

She rose up to sitting on his stomach. Her hair had lost its precise shape but the muss created a halo effect around her head. He licked the pad of his thumb and used it to lay down the fine line of blond hair between her mound and navel then he covered the smooth rosy peaks of her breasts with his warm hands. After a short rub, the buds perked again. He smiled.

Her head lilted pleasurably to one side. "I make you more sensual," she said.

He sighed briefly. "That you do."

"I dare say I also scare you." Her eyes followed the crown of his head down to his collarbone and chest, where her hands began to softly knead. "Few men can handle this intensity."

"I shall try," Athos said and acknowledged her massage with a few deep hums.

"You've passed several of my tests."

"Bravo for me, if you're the prize." He lightly rubbed her hips.

"Of course, it's been too long ago for you to remember them all," she said, kneading his pectoral muscles harder. "I told you when we first met that I needed to find out if you were good."

"As in, good *here*," he said and raced his hands up between her thighs.

She giggled, squirmed, and nodded. "And the next test was if you were giving."

"Giving, as in this," and he flicked a fingertip with his tongue twice and slipped it under the tuft of her mound. She instantly responded with a small shudder.

"Mm'yes," she said, eyes closed.

He would have continued playing with her sweet spot, but she scooted back. She looked happy but serious.

"The last test will be the most ... challenging." Her voice dropped an octave. "I want to know if you're game."

He tried to steal a kiss, but she leaned away. "Fere," she said, an edge to her voice, "we could live an even greater sensual life."

"I can't see how," he said, down on his back again, but not before he had devilishly raised an eyebrow.

She spread across his body so slowly and deliberately that every soft curve of her front moulded to his. No pockets of air separated them. Her lips touched his Adams apple and she licked a path from his throat to the underside of his chin. Arousal bolted through him. Again.

"Anne." He moaned. He wanted her. How many times could he want her in one night?

"If two hands are paradise," she said as her fingers caressed his hip, "then imagine what four could do."

And for an instant, he did, fantasising that Anne had doubled. But that was not what she meant.

He grabbed her hand from his side and lifted his head off the bed, an inch from her face. Her exhales swirled around his head, like the images of a third partner in their bed.

"I'm satisfied with *this* paradise," he said and the air turned hotter.

"You want me," she nodded, "and I want more."

"The subject is dead," he said and squeezed her hand. The musk of the sex they'd had filled his nostrils.

"Not for me." She moved her mouth to touch his lips but stopped short of a full kiss. "Fere, walk farther into the garden with me."

He kissed her because his need demanded it. In rushes of air through his nose, his chest filled and emptied in sync to black and white thoughts. Purity versus impurity. Despite her honesty and persistence, the picture of three promised only sin. His moral code rejected it. This proposition—her final test—broke the most fundamental religious principle he knew. Faithfulness.

"I cannot." His head fell back limp though his lips yearned for another kiss. "I married you in the eyes of God. You, Anne. Only you."

She rode up his body so that she sat steadfastly over his thumping heart. He wondered if she could feel its racing pulse between her legs.

"I would choose the right person for us." The way she spoke had a lushness so profound his body hummed with anticipation. But a thick slurry filled his brain.

Her voice muffled in his heavy head. "I have someone in

mind. Someone you know. Someone you trust. Someone right under your nose."

He sealed his eyes. But the image came anyway. Demi.

"No, no," he said, fighting the murky thoughts between his ears. Running a hand over his mouth, he murmured, "Never. Never would I consent. Neither would she."

Anne's breathing hitched, and she jerked up from his body. She found her legs and stood up to straddle him, a foot on each side of his waist. He'd awakened a beast. Her overpowering stance accused him of wrong, though her naked beauty tied him around her finger.

"None of this could end well," he said, reaching for her hand.

She locked his body between her feet like a vice. "Who is she?"

"No one like you," he said, knowing the right words didn't exist. "Anne, we cannot start down this road. No one would ever be right. You need to be the focal point of my attention, which is how it should be."

"But your mind immediately jumped to one person. A woman."

Athos skimmed up her calves from her stiff ankles. She never relaxed.

"I won't fight because of this." He dropped his hands and stretched out like a cross underneath her withering stare.

Tightly in control of her underlying rage, she knelt and peered over the top of his chest into his searching eyes. "No. You just don't know the rules. You assumed I meant like the picture in your book. Two women. One man." She shook her head.

His insides torqued. The tent became a dungeon.

As she reached for her clothes, Father Luc's last words raced forward: *Are there any signs or clues to confirm Bronte's story?*

She was dressed and at the canvas opening before he could put two coherent words together. He threw blankets aside and scrambled to his feet. A breeze through the flap hit him as she exited, and the early morning air added a cold layer onto his chilled skin.

"No, Anne," he called after her at the door. "You can't be serious."

Turning her head, the colour in her cheeks boiled to red. "It's best if you let me go for now. I have a new horse that needs riding." And she disappeared into the oncoming dawn.

Athos froze, waiting for a sign. Anne had flipped his world again. The snake ate its own tail. Disoriented, he dressed clumsily. He wasn't sure what to think or do. Could she possibly mean her brother? Even insinuating Bronte made his head spin. The lesser agony of the night was that Anne now knew his irreconcilable secret—that another woman haunted his thoughts.

A light wind outside the tent ruffled his loose shirttail. The sun had yet to rise fully above the trees. Starting out slowly, he took the path back to the main grounds. He was in no hurry to arrive home because he couldn't form a coherent response to Anne's idea. He needed a bottle to think.

When he came to the meadow, the slanted light from the sunrise struck the backside of the château at sharp angles. His boots darkened in the dew. The grass smelled of a fresh cut and brought on a vivid memory of last night's liberties.

He might always associate the smell of the outdoors now with their primitive behaviour. Maybe God meant the wild woods to be off limits, a Hell's gateway to the lowly beast inside a man. Myths and superstitions certainly supported that warning.

He sat in the grass. From here, he could see the main structures of Valliere from one corner to the other. The mansion, the outbuildings, the stables, and agricultural structures. His father's legacy. He wished he'd felt more than just a caretaker of it, wished he had grown into the role of sovereign before his father's death. Athos strained to fit into the framework but his strengths seemed mismatched.

He dropped his head to pray. It had been too long. He'd prayed at his confession to Father de Breuil but that day seemed long ago. He whispered a few incongruent lines. He needed a sign to understand who to believe, who to trust, and most importantly, who to love. The squeal of a horse snapped him out of it. In the grazing meadow, beyond shouting distance, he saw the Arabian and on its back was Anne.

The animal tousled and resisted her lead. It bucked and kicked. Riding astride in pants beneath a travelling dress, she dug her boots into the animal's sides, and Athos shot up from the grass, gasping as the stallion bucked again. But she held fast and whistled and yelled commands even he could hear. She wasn't backing down or flying off. She dominated the creature, much like she did everyone.

Athos waved, ready to call her name, but she galloped out of the fenced yard in the opposite direction, failing to see him. The stallion had given her the perfect excuse to leave for a while. For the first day since he'd married her, he felt truly alone.

"Take care," he said under his breath.

It occurred to him that he would miss her. It occurred to him that their push-and-pull might be the mortar of their relationship. It occurred to him to overlook everything, the evil pall, her outrageous request, and take her as she was. Seek peace in the turbulence. It occurred to him that he loved her. Little else made sense.

# Death Surrounds Her

Bright early sunlight and fatigue drove Athos indoors to his books. It seemed too early to drink, so he set aside the bottles of wine. In the library, he found the volume of Shakespeare on the chaise lounge, and it fell open to sonnet 135. He felt a kinship to the Englishman, one his fellow Frenchmen might snub. Regardless of the poet's unfortunate nationality, Athos believed the man's work spoke volumes. In 135, Shakespeare perfectly described Athos's predicament—obsessive love.

*Will in overplus. Will is large and spacious.*

His sexual appetite for Anne, his will, was outdone by her sexual appetite for all.

*Not once to hide my will in thine?*

Athos wanted his craven devotion to fill her as expansively

as it filled him. Maybe it could. He lay his listing head on the lounge and hoped, when she returned, it would.

•   •   •

"Wake up!"

Athos jolted up from his nap and switched from groggy to needle sharp without a breath. Unshaven and reeking of body odor, Bronte loomed over him. His usual handsomeness was drowned in shadow. Dark rings encircled his sunken eyes and his body sagged as would a snared rabbit hanging by its ears. His injured arm hung in a sling.

"She's dead." Bronte knotted his forehead into a gnarl of wrinkles.

Athos's mind jumped to the worst. *The Arabian threw Anne.*

Off his seat, Athos grabbed Bronte by the shoulders. "What happened?! Tell me!"

"She's dead." Bronte drew out the words through clenched teeth, punching out the last D. He rammed a fist into the lounge's cushion and shouted, "Dead, Athos!"

Athos flinched, praying the macabre message was a dream.

"Look at me," Athos insisted, squaring off. "Say everything."

"She drowned. In Agape Lake." Bronte's tear ducts glistened. "This morning."

Athos tottered back onto the lounge. He tried forming Anne's name on his parched lips, but his voice dried up. The music of her stopped playing. The poetry of her stopped repeating. The beauty of her ceased to exist.

"*Say something!*" Bronte demanded, his voice cracking. "*If you don't, I shall go mad!*"

"Who found her?"

"A peasant from the village."

"Where is she?"

"Her body is in Father Luc's care at the cathedral." Bronte gaped at his shaking hands, white and empty. Tremors worked their way up his body. "You know why I'm here."

Dismayed, Athos's dull gaze came to rest on Bronte's cutting, anger-filled eyes.

Bronte brought out a dagger from the hip of his belt. "Demi couldn't swim."

*Demi? Not Anne.*

*Demi. Dead.*

Athos buckled over and held his head between his knees. The realisation slammed into him like the clap of a hammer on a missionary bell. His whole body vibrated and a death gong clanged inside his head. Tolling tolling tolling.

*Demi drowned. And Bronte and I will drown without her.*

Bronte carved the silence open. "Where's Anne?"

Athos drew up his head and glanced toward the picture window. "Gone." He barely recognised his own voice.

"Where did she go?" Bronte pointed the dagger aggressively north, south, east then west.

"I ... I don't know."

"You don't know?" Bronte's good arm flew up. "He doesn't know! The lord of Valliere is not the master of his castle!" Bronte hit the sarcastic notes with supreme accuracy. "My sovereign has lost track of his wife."

"Tell me Demi isn't gone." Athos's shoulder blades ached and the gong drummed on in his brain and numbed his extremities and his ability to think.

"You have no right to mourn her!" Bronte accused. "She was never yours. You confused her and made her doubt her real affections for me. For me! Your betrayal is beyond comprehension." Bronte snarled and approached Athos, dagger first. "The smell of the dung heaps is sweeter than your bleeding heart. Your colossal self-absorption stains everything you've touched lately. Wake up! Anne's gone. Demi's dead. Dead! Death surrounds your wife, my lord, and you'll be next if you don't open your eyes."

Athos throbbed from head to heel. Tolling tolling tolling. He imagined water filling Demi's mouth and lungs, smothering the life from her beautiful bosom. His hands had not been there to rescue her. They had been preoccupied. His whole life, preoccupied. The cruelty suffocated his conscience.

Bronte levelled the dagger at Athos's line of sight. "If you don't doubt Anne now, you're a damned fool."

"Even if I knew where she went this morning," Athos rasped from his dry throat, "this can't be."

"It is. And I'm going to hunt and kill her."

Athos grabbed Bronte's wrist. The dagger wavered between them in a tense tug of war. "She's my wife. She's protected by my rule."

"Look at you, such a pathetic, small man. What will you do to make it all right for yourself now?" To top off his sardonic tirade, Bronte broke the hold Athos had on the dagger. "You won't stop me, Athos, and if you try, you'll have to kill me first."

Bronte got halfway to the door before Athos tackled him to the floor. Landing on his injured arm, Bronte screamed and cursed.

Athos held him down by a knee. "Justice is mine to seek."

Bronte scowled in pain from the body slam. "I don't need you to seek it!"

Dread wrapped around Athos's spine like a poisonous serpent. "I'll find her," Athos said, lifting himself off Bronte's back, "so it comes down to this."

Bronte pushed up on his good elbow to get off the floor. Floundering, he flopped over, sweaty on his upper lip, and grimaced to stand up. "You can't stop me from going after her, too. I'll never rest."

Athos stepped back and detested the future, which hinged on hunting a woman. The outcome, either truth or death.

# The Final Hunt

"You're wrong about her, and you know it!" Bronte started chiding Athos as soon as the two burst out the front doors of Valliere. Athos wanted to swat him like a horsefly, but Bronte stalked him outside, and as he did prior to every sport they'd played, Bronte taunted from the get-go. "You doubt her. You've seen the Devil in her. I can tell."

Athos walked faster as they neared the stables. As calmly as he could, he said, "You won't be able to keep up because of your injury."

Bronte gritted his teeth, hugging the sling, and rebounded. "No thanks to you." He darted out in front and began walking backward to face Athos, who kept his eyes on the ground. "Tell me," Bronte urged, "all the things she's done to make you wonder. Odd behaviour. Stories that reveal her true nature."

*Of course. Everything.* But Athos didn't want to think. He wanted the chaos to end. The doubts, the fighting. And especially, the dying. Bile burned the back of his throat. Finding his anger, Athos confronted Bronte at the threshold of the stable entrance. "How did we get here? You introduced me to Anne. You encouraged me to take her on as a sexual challenge. Then you muddied the waters. Not me. Not her. You fell for her and ran away to find reasons to hate her."

"That's what she wants you to believe, Athos. She's manipulative and says what she wants to get what she wants."

"And therefore we blame her for the death of Demi? What does she have to gain by killing Demi?" Athos choked out the sentence. He could hardly believe sweet Demi was gone. If it weren't for his need to find Anne, he'd be immobile with grief.

"Maybe nothing." Bronte said, the wind gone from his argument. "Maybe nothing at all."

In front of them in the stable, Zahn appeared toting a saddle. "She said you might be coming out soon." Zahn nodded toward Athos.

"Who said?" Athos and Bronte blurted simultaneously.

"The comtesse."

Athos stepped closer to the old man. "She's been here? When?"

"Not long ago. Within the half hour. She said she wanted to take a longer ride and needed provisions."

Bronte pulled Athos back by the shoulder. "Her coming back doesn't prove anything." Bronte pushed him a little. "If she's killed Demi, she's on the run. Why else would she leave you behind?"

Athos shook his head to clear his senses. Bronte's one-track mind astonished him. Bronte was still trying to save him. "At least it won't be hard to catch up with her and find out."

Athos's horse was saddled and ready before Bronte fetched his from the gatehouse. Athos took off down a back meadow ahead of Bronte, who lagged several horse lengths behind. The search for Anne represented the classic hunt between old rivals. Headstrong and competitive, each hunter would jockey for an advantage. Athos wasn't interested in being sportsmanlike. On this hunt, there would be no friendly gestures.

"She'll just fill your head with lies," yelled Bronte, who slapped his horse double-time but fell farther behind. The men thundered across the field. The static earth was their stage.

"Don't follow me!" Athos snaked his steed through a dry creek bed and over to the other side. Steering in jerks, Bronte pressed the chase. The pebbles in the creek crunched loudly under hot pursuit. Athos couldn't shake Bronte, just like he couldn't shake the sorrow over Demi. Just like he couldn't escape the questions that pushed him to find his wife.

She had been gone the entire morning, the morning of Demi's death. *Why?* She had returned and left again without waking him. *Why? Their argument?* He could only guess at her motives. Today, once and for all, he needed the truth.

Finding a shortcut, Athos aimed for a dense wood in the direction of her brother's church. The ride there was too long for leisure, but Anne might take it to try out her new horse. Paradoxically, he hoped she'd gone elsewhere. He didn't want to see Father de Breuil. *Someone you know. Someone right under your nose.* He'd ignored the clues too long.

Hurling his horse into the dark green between the trees, Athos galloped through the woods, lush and thick with moss, lichen, ferns, vines and laurels. By horseback, he knew the dips in the land the way he knew Anne's body. The curves would obscure his tracks. Here, he found cover from Bronte. With Anne, he'd momentarily found cover from pain.

Athos threw out caution and sped up rather than slowed down. The sound of Bronte at his heels dropped to a distant thrum. Athos streaked through narrow passageways; trees whipped by, and the woods blurred after each whip.

His heart pounded until it was so loud he knew it was more than the sound of his blood pumping. Ahead of him, another set of hooves was covering ground. His instincts had been on target.

"Anne!" Her name flew back in his face. "Anne!"

Strike after strike, he wielded the whip. Horse sweat splattered from the leather cords onto his pants. The three-beat gait of the mysterious rider far in front of him jumped to four. Now, Athos, the pursuer, had found his target.

He wanted her to stop. He wanted her to come to him. He wanted a resolution, but he fell behind. If the horse in front of him was the Arabian, it flaunted its superiority. Athos's hopes flagged as did his horse's energy and zeal for the chase. Devastated, he pulled back on the reins rather than risk his horse collapsing. Slowing to a trot and then a full stop, he listened.

A blunt thud sounded in the trees, and the incessant rhythm of the lead horse ceased. Athos dismounted, and his heart changed to ice. Seconds passed. In the corner of his vision, the gift he'd given to Anne, the creamy Arabian stallion from a foreign land, appeared in the periphery. Without its rider.

"My lady!" Athos shouted. "My lady!"

Silence.

His frozen heart cracked.

Remounting, Athos frantically hurtled toward the scared Arabian and scanned the forest floor, calling out her name. Once, twice, a dozen times, but nothing.

"*Hah-ya!*"

His horse sprinted to high speed and ripped at the ground cover. He caught no trace of her—neither loose lace nor lost ribbons. His head spun in all directions. Fifty yards and no sign. One hundred yards and emptiness.

The caw of a crow broke his fever. He rallied in its direction and spotted colour in the grass. Her lavender dress. Below an oak, Anne lay curled and unconscious. From his horse, he wailed from his tight chest. She didn't move.

Panicked, he dismounted and tumbled to his knees a few yards away. All legs and arms, he scrambled toward her crumpled heap. Her head was slack atop a bed of moss. Brambles stuck to her hair, dirt soiled a cheek, and blood streaked a chambray sleeve. Her limb twisted at the shoulder, disjointed. She groaned slowly, low inside her.

"Say you are with me!" he begged.

He brushed her face and pleaded for her to wake. Her body and the bloody arm were limp. As he lifted the limb, one rushing breath escaped her, but she stayed below surface.

A prayer formed in his speechless throat. *What next God? Show mercy.*

At the bloody half-sleeve, he swiftly ran his hunting knife. By chance or fate or in reply to his prayer, the black ribbon tied to her arm, her symbol of mourning, sliced in two.

Beneath the severed tag, a purplish scar marred her near-perfect skin.

*The brand of a fleur-de-lis.*

The mark of a criminal blazed in his eyes.

The unmistakable evidence. Horrific. Permanent. Hidden.

His face sank. Thoughts scattered. Nerves coursed.

He rubbed his thumbs over the indelible mark, pressing deeply, driven by truth. *Be gone like dirt.* Nausea built inside him. He pressed deeper, hard enough to bruise her, still pressing until scratches below the brand oozed blood.

Backing off, he hung his head between his shoulders. All Bronte's warnings came rushing in and the rotten smell of death surrounded him. Father Turre's. Demi's. His soul's. Somewhere inside him, the broken animal howled.

•　　•　　•

In the echo of his own scream, he disconnects. He feels nothing. Time stops.

She stirs. Her face creases; the damage sets in. Though a few feet away, he does not reach for her.

She rasps, "Fere. Fere, my love."

Anger stings his eyes. She sees her exposed brand and gasps, recoils and flounders to her feet. He teeters on the precipice of sanity, wants her to suffer, throws stones of accusations.

"What are you?!" he says, nay explodes. "A thief, a whore? A murderer?!"

She falls into the oak, turning her face into its rough bark.

He bellows. "WHY? Why this? I looked away for everything!"

She whimpers, refuses to speak.

His mind collapses into senselessness, a blurry mish-mash of their past.

"Everything Bronte says is true." His lips move without feeling. "You've deceived me, and I let you."

Her muscles tense to *flee*.

He moves with the steadiness of an executioner. He takes a rope from his saddle. Knots bind her wrists, bloodied by his hard hands. Then he wrangles the skittish Arabian and secures the other end of the rope to the beast's stiff leather stirrup.

He spews coarse words and flails his arms. And, lastly, he strikes his leather whip on the backside of the terrified horse. Like a spark from Hell, the stallion tears through the brambles, dragging her weight.

Her agony is deafening. Shrieks collide with hoof beats. The windows of his life shatter.

He watches, unmoved, while his soul and the criminal cross into Purgatory.

He waits, long and still, for the forest to quiet.

But under the canopy of a black dawn, Anne's once-sweet voice haunts the oncoming dark.

*Fere. Fere, my love.*

# 29

# His Separation

Athos had no idea how long he stood motionless in the woods under the oak.

"Athos," Bronte called from the trees. "Athos? Do you hear me?"

Athos dropped the whip and a brushing noise on the forest floor pulled his stare downward. A long black snake slithered over the toe of his boot and into a dark hole at the base of the oak.

"You did what you had to do." Had Bronte already said this once? Fifty times? Had he been a witness?

For a short distance, Athos walked the cut the Arabian had left in its wake. The human anchor it had raked across the ground left upturned slashes of brown soil. He saw it as the line he'd crossed. The evidence of his downturn. The on-set of life as a damaged man.

His doing. And God's.

Athos uttered semi-coherently both a statement and a question. "She never cried for mercy."

"Because she was guilty." Bronte clutched the back of Athos's neck, maybe in an attempt to make the declaration truer. Or less painful. The gesture didn't undo anything.

Bronte gave him a shake. "It's done. It's over."

Blankly, Athos rocked his head from side to side until he shook it, as if casting off a bad dream. "Her brother." He grabbed Bronte's arm over his shoulder and came around. "And you're wrong. It's not over. It's just beginning. Go get him."

# From Eden to Inferno

As soon as Bronte left to collect Father de Breuil, Athos rode, dazed, back to Valliere. His interior compass awry, Athos emerged from the woods an hour later on the cusp of evening. From the edge of his meadow, everything at Valliere looked different. More specifically, he saw it through the warped lens of the short life he had once shared with Anne.

In the middle of the grazing field, he dismounted and removed the reins of his horse. He unbuckled the martingale straps and yanked the saddle to the ground. He slapped the horse, and it veered toward a group of mares, far away from the phantom who had been riding it.

Unwavering, he stared at the tops of his boots, which shushed in the grass as he walked. Each step took him closer to disillusion. He'd worn the shoes into paradise and now into the depths of something so pitch black he could not see out of it.

He had little recollection of arriving inside the stable. Athos stood by the empty stall of the Arabian, waiting. His mind muted sight and sound. His heartbeat became incoherent, and emptiness coated him along with her blood on his hands and a stinging rope burn on one palm.

Air abandoned him. Reason abandoned him. Hope abandoned him.

He could not understand. But he did remember.

He bent over and retched the hollowness out of his stomach. He faltered, fell forward, and caught a post before sprawling onto his shins in the dust. He dug the heels of his hands into his eyes and bellowed from an expanding blackness within.

•　　•　　•

Lost, he wandered inside the château. The wine from Anne sat on a side table in the library, mocking him. He dumped the contents in the kitchen compost, took three bottles from his own cellar, and moved the wound-licking to the banquet room.

The blades of the Musketeer swords twinkled in the candlelight on the long table. Athos stopped at each one, turned it over twice, and stepped to the next. He drank straight from the bottle as he moved down the line. At the last one, Bronte tumbled through the double doors, breathless.

"Thank God you're here," Bronte said and pulled off his gloves.

Athos kept his calculating eye on Father Luc's collection and drank in long swallows.

"Father de Breuil is gone." Bronte spoke in an outpour. "The talk all over Averdon is that he quit the parish and left this morning. There's nothing left in the church's collection or strongbox. The village is in an uproar. They sent me to tell Father Luc, but I wanted to tell you first."

Athos started his inspection of the swords again, turning each blade twice then moving to the next. He wiped wine off his mouth with the back of his hand.

"Athos!" Bronte slammed his hand down on the next sword in line. "Are you listening?"

Athos's grey eyes met Bronte's searing ones. Without firing off, Athos said, "The church coffers aren't the only ones empty."

"What?"

"My family treasure. All the heirlooms." Taking another swig, he tipped the bottle so far back that he faced the ceiling.

"Gone?"

"My casket is empty. My family documents were burned in the bedroom fireplace."

Bronte stumbled backward. "Your wealth."

"Did you track de Breuil?" Athos asked, eerily calm, and picked up a sword that was missing a tip.

"No, I was too worried."

"Hmm." Athos nodded and put his bottle on the table to fixate on the weapon.

"I was worried about you," Bronte reiterated.

No answer.

"Athos," Bronte said as he pushed the blade down from Athos's studied gaze using the outside of his forearm. In both hands, Bronte took him by the neck. "Look at me and tell me what's going on inside your head."

Athos slid the sword back on the table and smoothed his friend's arms down. He steadied them both. "Demi is dead because of me."

Bronte shook his head, slowly then vigorously. "You didn't kill her. Anne did."

"Anne knew about my affections for Demi all along because I confessed them to her brother."

"You did what?" Bronte craned his ear forward.

"The day before our wedding, I chose to confess to her brother instead of Father Luc."

"But if Anne knew about Demi from the beginning—"

"Anne must have been convinced she'd conquered my affections during the month we were here alone. God would have sworn she had. Except that I still had feelings for Demi." Athos stared off, empty-eyed. "It was too late by then. Anne had fallen in love with me. Once she realised I was torn, it ignited her jealousy. A deadly jealousy."

Bronte opened his mouth, but no sound came out.

"I'm leaving Valliere," Athos said and stood back to review the swords. His placid expression didn't jibe with any of the words spilling out. "You'll help me. I want everything burned. All the furniture, my clothes, the linens ... the books." Expressionless, he glanced from one end of the room to the other and from floor to ceiling. "You must find the Arabian and her body, then burn them, too. You'll tell everyone I died in the fire and that Anne died with me. I'm leaving a document that grants you my sovereignty upon my death."

Bronte's head had started shaking again at the word *burned* and had not stopped. "You can't let her do this to you!"

"It'll be up to you to re-establish a residence for the sovereignty somewhere in Berry. This is the most important responsibility I'll ever place on you, may *ever* place on you again." Athos started to reach for the bottle.

"No. No! I won't do it!" Bronte swung his arms wildly across the table and knocked the bottle over and several swords out of place.

Athos carefully re-aligned each blade of steel and righted the bottle, though the wine had spilled.

"She's not worth giving up everything for," Bronte argued, though Athos was a blank wall. "You can't make this decision today—after what happened in the woods."

"I broke with myself, Bronte. There's nothing I can do to redeem this situation—or myself."

"You didn't cause this. She did! She seduced you. She seduced me. She duped us both and wreaked all this havoc. She always planned to take what she could. You can't blame yourself for being tricked by the Devil."

"But I can take responsibility." Athos moved to the head of the table. "There's no peace for me here. Everywhere I turn, I see her. Even here." On the polished wood, he spread out the fingers of one hand, beneath which laid a glorious, but now tainted, memory of Anne. "If you won't burn the place to the ground, I will."

After a pause, Bronte said desperately, "Your books."

Athos removed his hand from the table. "I'd burn every word in print if it meant Demi could live."

A flaming wick popped from a candle in the room.

Knowing he'd aimed at Bronte's most vulnerable spot, Athos watched his oldest friend fold, but not on the outside. A long silence confirmed his acquiescence. Before Bronte could change his mind, Athos took two small items from a buffet table and handed them over.

In Bronte's cold hands, Athos placed his journal and the book of Shakespeare. "Start the fire with these."

"When?"

"After Demi's funeral Mass."

• • •

The next morning, Athos took his place as sovereign in the front pew of the cathedral beside Demi's whimpering mother, stoic father, and two inconsolable sisters. Directly behind him, Bronte sat bolstered between his father and brother. Bronte's mother was too aggrieved to attend the Mass.

Dressed in a stiff, ornately embroidered formal suit, Athos sat erect and his eyes bore down on the casket a few feet in front of him. The rope burn underneath his glove stung. The sickeningly strong incense in the swinging thurible coated his throat. Yet he willed his arms and legs to be still, head forward, eyes dry. He had honed his self-control by fencing. Why he'd lost control in the woods confounded him. Shadowed him. *Will haunt me until I choose not to live.*

His heart was split open. Throughout the service—the prayers, the wails—his chest flooded with sorrow. The breach widened following each incantation of Father Luc.

**"Abiit nemine salutata."** *She went away without bidding anyone farewell.*

How much grief could one man survive? Was Athos so

arrogant to think that the despair and guilt wracking him outdid the suffering of the world's nameless minions? If it did, he would gladly shoulder the end of the world.

He took no comfort in Father Luc's rituals nor the pageantry of the Mass. As the service closed and the sobs flowed underneath his ruminations, Athos believed he'd never find comfort in God again. Because God, in all His power, had abandoned him. The evidence, shrouded and silent, lay in a long brown box, sprinkled with holy water.

# Last Rites

Athos waited an hour after the burial to go back to the cathedral. Under his arm, he brought a thick, round canvas bundle tied by two wide, leather straps. Wrapped inside, Father Luc's swords clinked together.

The priest sat, head down, in the same place Athos had occupied during the service. Athos almost turned back and would have had the priest not spoken.

"Come in," Father Luc called out, face forward.

Athos readjusted the heavy bundle under his arm and re-affirmed his purpose. There was much to be said before he could set his final plan in motion.

Father Luc gave him a head-to-toe inspection as soon as Athos fixed his heels to the floor in front of him.

"You made it," Father Luc said.

Athos's forehead puckered in confusion.

"You made it through the service with your dignity intact," the priest clarified. "That's more than I can say for Bronte."

Frustrated, Athos frowned and shot a short puff of air through his nose.

"What do you have there?" Father Luc pointed to the bundle.

Athos rolled the canvas onto the pew and undid the ties. Several of the better swords were wrapped in silk. He took the finest one out of its silky cover and turned it over a few times under a tall ray of red light coming from a stained-glassed window.

"I have need of your services," Athos said, becoming entranced by the silvery flash of the blade. Seeing it shine made his doubts about his next steps vanish.

"On any ordinary day, I'd oblige. But if you've come to convince me to give you a sword lesson, you'll be sorely disappointed," the priest said and started to scoot off the pew.

Athos pointed the sword above the V in Father Luc's robe below the throat. The priest let all the air out of his lungs and sagged as the stress of the morning settled on his shoulders.

"Haven't we done this once before? Put my sword away," he said and raised a cantankerous eyebrow. "It's been an extremely difficult morning, which I believe you can appreciate, and I have no desire for games right now."

"I'm not playing a game," Athos said and pressed the tip a little more into the target.

"But you're acting like a child."

"I sat right there this morning where you sit now and listened and prayed and chanted on cue, my emotions under check, my face flat as paper, while the entire time my heart was being carved out."

Father Luc opened his mouth to speak but Athos butted in. "Don't get confused. This isn't a confession. I'm finished with religious dogma and the obligations of this place where I was supposed to find perfection and peace and the answers to life. I've discovered God is flawed. And terribly cruel."

Again, Father Luc tried to say something, only to be shut down as quickly as before.

"You were right about one thing, though, Father Luc. I was in love with Demi. I tried convincing myself I wasn't. Made every attempt to cast her from my thoughts and justify my feelings, but mostly, I failed." Athos reached for a second sword in the pile and pointed them both at the priest, who now looked more than a little concerned. "But I also realised that I loved Anne beyond reason and certainly beyond purity. God was testing me. And I wrestled with guilt and desire because despite my folly, I loved two women. How could God be so tortuous? I couldn't think of a single biblical story that would allow me the right to have them both. Ah, but perhaps a man of lesser morals would have found one, especially an aristocrat. Henry the Eighth wrote the book. My nobility be damned, I chose the path of righteousness, and I picked one woman over the other."

"The wrong one," Father Luc said, his voice turning downward.

"What about love is wrong or right?" Athos tossed his head and jangled the swords. "I went from none to too much." He aligned the swords, resting the tips on Father Luc's frock across his chest. "Now, after all those problems, my arms are empty."

"But Anne—"

"Anne is dead."

Father Luc fell back in the seat and blubbered a few lines of a common prayer.

"Yes, old man, say her a prayer. No one else will."

Crossing himself, Father Luc turned his confusion outward. "How could this be?"

"By my own hands," Athos said and swivelled his wrists and the swords at the same time. "Your doubts about her were very foretelling."

Father Luc crossed himself again.

"She harboured an evilness inside her that ate away her goodness. I think she wanted to be free of it. Sometimes, during our most intimate moments, she let it go. But she'd been ruined and couldn't break from her past. I see her now for what she is ... was. To save her would have wiped away every shred of my honour. Destroying her almost did."

Father Luc raised his hand, but Athos tapped it with his sword. The priest returned his hand to its place on the bench. "If you've killed an innocent woman," Father Luc said, "even if she wasn't innocent, you need to ask God for forgiveness."

"I killed her because God made it impossible for any other outcome." Athos sighed. "And that's what brings me back to you."

Athos turned the pommel of a sword toward the priest. Father Luc looked at it as if it were a stolen loaf of bread.

"Take it." Athos bumped him in the chest with it.

"What on earth for?"

"I want to see if I can best a Musketeer."

Father Luc sputtered and coughed until he bent over, red in the face. "You want what?"

"A duel."

"Listen, my son—"

"A duel or a slit throat. You have ten seconds."

"This either ends with you killing an old priest or an old priest killing you, neither of which sounds very honourable."

"Eight."

"And what if I win?" Father Luc commanded the sword.

"You live."

The priest harrumphed. "You're impossible."

With three seconds to spare, the duel was on.

•　　•　　•

The silence that had draped the cathedral clattered alive with swordplay. Athos executed unorthodox feints and attacks that Father Luc defended in blinking speed. Twice the priest nearly took Athos's iron, but his grip held and Athos backed off and paced in a tight circle to regroup. That, and the speed of their exchanges, made Father Luc beam.

"Ha!" the priest blurted, loosening a tie at the waist of his clerical robes. "Thought you'd dash me off before we even got started."

The priest fought as if he were a master of his own style of fencing. Several times, he swung his belly into the fight and pushed his weight around to throw Athos off balance. Athos ticked off all the tricks he had in his practice book. None goaded, flustered, or tripped up his opponent.

"I know what you're up to," Father Luc said, less winded than Athos. "You want to see if you have what it takes to be a Musketeer."

Athos lunged with an overhead slam. Blocked again. Rage scratched at the base of his scalp. "Wrong!"

"Now I see it in your eyes," Father Luc said, a little too cockily. "You have dreams of infamy rambling 'round your head."

"Wrong!" Athos fell into the priest, shoving him into a pedestal full of pewter candlesticks. The wood column toppled over and the two on top of it. The pewter clanged and bounced across the stone floor.

Athos was the first on his feet. "Get up! Try again."

Father Luc rocked his broad belly this way and that until he sat upright. He shot up his hand for a lift. Athos refused.

Grumbling, the priest shoved himself to his feet and stood down. "What are we doing?"

"Duelling," Athos said and raised his sword.

"Until you tell me what this is all about, I believe I'll sit out the fight."

But as soon as the priest began to turn toward the pews, Athos grabbed a handful of robe beneath Father Luc's chin. "Raise your sword and fight."

"You've been under extreme duress," the priest said, hardening his face. "You should rethink your strategy."

Athos shoved the priest backward and flung his sword around. The momentum threw Athos forward. Father Luc blocked the low swing with his blade and wrenched Athos by the neck onto his back on the floor. Stepping in Athos's armpit, the priest settled his swordtip under Athos's ribcage.

"Over now?"

Athos squirmed, and the priest leaned in.

"You could ask for mercy," the priest suggested.

Athos turned his cheek to the cold stone floor. A sword in his belly would end the heartbreak and take no more out of him than he'd already lost. Plan accomplished. "Make it clean."

In the heavy quiet, Father Luc flapped an exasperated groan from his lips. "Well, sometimes I'm wrong." He lifted the sword from Athos's middle and offered a hand. Athos didn't move, but he heard the priest shuffle over to the pew and sit.

Father Luc sighed. "Now I understand why you're here."

Athos could almost hear the priest shaking his head.

"You're a good swordsman, Athos. It would be a shame—not to mention a sin—for me to kill you."

"I'm still breathing."

"For now. If you want to die, you'll find a way." The light in the room dimmed as a few of the candles from the service flickered out. "You'll suffer forever if you don't forgive yourself first, whether or not you seek mercy from God."

The wake of events washed over Athos. He wanted a different life but forgiveness seemed a worthless exercise. "I'll always have blood on my hands."

"I'm not talking about feeling responsible for Demi's death or forgiving yourself for killing Anne," Father Luc said. "You'll need to forgive yourself for loving her."

Athos looked up at the ceiling, the beamed domes, and floral reliefs in gold.

Father Luc looked up, too. "Your pain is recent. Give yourself time. Give yourself a new purpose. The longer you commiserate with your pain, the less likely you'll outlive it."

"How long?"

"It may not be a matter of *when*, but *who* will help you overcome this." Father Luc pushed off the bench and headed for his study. "Follow me."

Athos took his time getting up. Alone in the cathedral, he wondered if any person could convince him to trust his feelings of love again. He, himself, could not.

Father Luc sat at his desk scribbling a note when Athos came in several minutes later. Rather than sit, Athos waited by the door. His time here, in any church, was winding down.

"Bronte tells me you're going away," Father Luc said, glancing up and back down.

"I asked for his confidence."

"Be gentle on him. Compared to you, the last few days have had the opposite spiritual effect on him. I lose one, gain another." Father Luc chuckled straight from his ample belly. "Going to Paris?"

Athos nodded.

"I knew it." The priest ended his note with a flourish. "I have a name for you, someone who'll help you settle in and find good pursuits. He's a young Musketeer but he's considering the priesthood."

Athos took the note, read it, and stuffed it in his pocket. "I'll take it only because he's a Musketeer."

"You're welcome," Father Luc said, sucking in his cheeks against a smile. "You may also keep my sword. You might need it."

Athos had forgotten he was still holding it. Bringing the steel forward, he decided to let the priest feel good about something. "Thank you."

Their farewell was brief. Avoiding the open square, Athos took a side exit into an alley where his horse awaited, packed for the trip, a journey he thought Father Luc's sword might have spared him. He mounted and idled, giving the village one last look behind him. Before riding out, he took the note from his pocket and read the name again.

*At the Rue Servandoni, find this trustworthy man, the Vicomte d'Aramitz, also known as Aramis.*


THE END

# Athos's Last Log Entry

*I have witnessed Hell with mortal eyes. She will haunt me through my final days. The sun shall never rise.*

# The Lost Papers of Athos

*Bronte's Poem for Demi*
*by Athos*
You bind me to love,
Taming me with gentle winds,
My sails, my course, my desire.
Be mine.

•   •   •

*Athos's Poem to Anne*
If soils falter and the world fails,
In your search, I will fly.
On thy beauty, I will alight.
For thy love, I will fight.
Against thy breast, I will be still.
Forsaking the end and God's will.

# Bronte's Letter to Athos, Two Months After His Departure to Paris

*My dear friend, we have boarded up the charred shell of Valliere and burned her contents. The blaze lasted three days, and the locals took it as a bad omen. Unfortunately, we never found the Arabian or Anne's body. A spectacular funeral Mass was held in your honour, led by Father Luc. He filled it with many kind remarks about you. For a small sum, my father, brother, and I have purchased the Castle de Bragelonne, which was behind on rents. Our family has taken up residence there until such time that you return. I'm confident you will someday take your rightful place here. In anticipation, we will continue to speak well of the sovereign we once knew as Athos. Find your peace.*

# Acknowledgments

This story benefits from the advice of many wonderful people. My endearing thanks to Stephen Parolini and Taylor Sisk, whose careful reads kept my story out of a lot of trouble and improved readability and believability. My Portland, Ore., critique group, Marlene Hill Taevs, Linda Smith, and D'Norgia Taylor-Price, provided invaluable plot and scene suggestions, all in gentle, humour-filled sessions over the course of a very difficult year in my life. I also thank my mother, Carol Fulford, and my cousin, Rebecca Rupard Green, for reading early drafts and encouraging my journey. To my children, wait until you're twenty to read the story of *Athos and Milady*, then you can give mom the ol' slant eye. Touché.

www.TheMusketeerSeries.com

www.ingramcontent.com/pod-product-compliance
Lightning Source LLC
Chambersburg PA
CBHW070535120726